MURDER BY MOONLIGHT

A Windswept Book

WINDSWEPT TITLES
FROM SCHOLASTIC

Don't Walk Alone by Mary Bringle
Someone Is Out There by Carole Standish
Girl in the Shadows by Miriam Lynch
The House of Three Sisters by Virginia Nielsen
Yesterday's Girl by Madeline Sunshine
The Snow's Secret by Carole Standish
The Red Room by Kaye Dobkin
The Silvery Past by Candice Ransom
Dreams and Memories by Lavinia Harris
A Forgotten Girl by Elisabeth Ogilvie
The Ghost of Graydon Place by Dorothy Francis
The Silent Witness by Meredith Hill
The Empty Attic by Jean Francis Webb
Murder by Moonlight by Dorothy Woolfolk

MURDER BY MOONLIGHT

Dorothy Woolfolk

SCHOLASTIC BOOK SERVICES
New York Toronto London Auckland Sydney Tokyo

Cover Photo by Owen Brown

ISBN 0-590-32438-1

 Published by Scholastic Book Services, a division of Scholastic Inc.

12 11 10 9 8 7 6 5 4 3 2 1 3 3 4 5 6/8

Printed in the U. S. A. 06

For Jane Ann Cross

MURDER BY MOONLIGHT

A Windswept Book

CHAPTER 1

"Here comes the weirdo again," Kristin Mulroy said. "I can't stand him."

Beside her in the airplane seat, Alexa Bower snorted. "He's only trying to be helpful, Kristin. Like a good steward is supposed to be." She nodded her head toward the young English steward who was making his way down the aisle, carrying several magazines.

He stopped beside their seat and said, "Hello, again." Then he grimaced and bent down to pick up Kristin's dark brown tote bag at her feet.

"This seems to be in your way. I'll stow it up above, or" — he indicated the front of the plane — "I can put it safely away in the luggage compartment."

Kristin took the bag from him and put it back on the floor. "It's not in my way, thank you."

"Good, then. As long as you're comfortable." He smiled and held a magazine out toward her. As she shook her head, he said, "No? Well, we've got quite a good film this trip. It features your own Christopher Reeve. How about it, ladies? Shall I get you some earphones?"

Kristin sat immobile. Alexa said quickly, "Not just now. It's terribly nice of you to ask." She beamed at him and tried to sound British.

"Not-at-all!" he said in a rapid-fire delivery that came out as one word with a little explosive *pop!* at the end. He looked warmly at the two girls, then disappeared down the aisle to the kitchen quarters in the rear.

"Why is he picking on us?" Kristin said, staring after him. "What's all that about my tote bag?"

Alexa smoothed her dark, shining hair and smirked. "It's because we're two good-looking American girls, at least according to him. The kind that type of Englishman really flips out over."

Kristin looked at her disdainfully. "I can't believe you, Alexa. This guy isn't flirting with us. I'm trying to tell you that he's up to something. I only wish I knew what it is."

At that moment, the plane dipped low and was immersed in a white snow-cloud world above the Atlantic Ocean.

Kristin, forgetting her anxiety, yelled, "Look! Isn't that sensational?"

Alexa yawned and patted the cushion behind her head into place. "Kristin, please! I was up half the night, packing. I'm going to take a nap. Good night."

She turned her head away, leaving Kristin with her thoughts.

I know there's something wrong with that man, Kristin brooded. Something . . . mysterious.

Like her mother's letter, received one short week ago. The letter that had set her off on this terrific trip to England. She withdrew it from her purse and reread the part that puzzled her:

> *". . . so I'll be off to Yorkshire on what may very well prove to be a wild goose chase for a few days before I come down to London. (I've spoken to the Bowers and they're arranging for Alexa to fly with you. They have to take a later plane.) So just be patient, darling. I'll tell you everything when I meet you in London. I'll probably be getting into Victoria Station at seven o'clock on Saturday night — the three-thirty train from Leeds. I know that gives you a day in London with the Bowers, but I'm sure you'll have a lovely time just sightseeing. If I can get down any sooner, you know I will. In any case, I'll give you a call.*
>
> *What I'm tracking down is a long shot, I'll admit. If the papers prove to be the real thing, well, my dearest daughter, I can rip up my thesis and set the world of literature on its ears. All I can say is that it's about my favorite authors, the Brontës — Charlotte Brontë, actually . . ."*

What was her mother talking about? Why all the mystery? Oh, well, it didn't matter. She was on her way to London, the biggest trip away from Indiana she'd ever taken. She'd find out everything tomorrow, Saturday, when her mother arrived at the Daley.

She settled back in her seat. She would not let

anything bother her. Not even Harold, the dopey steward, with his peculiar way of stopping by and bothering them with his helpful hints that they didn't want or need. Alexa was happily sleeping. Kristin looked out the round porthole into the banked mass of snow-white clouds outside. She sighed contentedly.

But she would not have felt so serene if she could have seen the young English steward in the rear of the plane, staring at the two girls up front with calculating blue eyes.

As the bus tooled along the London streets, Alexa, in the window seat, squealed with pleasure at the passing scene.

"Aren't they wonderful? The English! They even look different from Americans!"

"They really do. What I love are the names on those stores." Kristin leaned across Alexa at the window. " 'Forby's Tea Shoppe,' 'Wimpy's Hamburgers,' 'The Mysterious Bookshop.' "

"Look at that sign on the gas station," Alexa said. " 'Petrol, £1.59.' " She giggled. "My deah, isn't it too, too divine?"

The bus jolted to a stop in front of a huge, old, red brick building — the Hotel Daley. The two girls got out and walked to the side of the bus where the driver was unloading luggage.

"And which is your bag, young lady?" he asked.

"The striped one — tan and dark green." Alexa flashed him a bright smile.

Beside her, something made Kristin look up at the bus window. Her heart lurched. There he was again! The steward! *He's been riding on the same bus with us! And now he's getting off at our stop, our hotel!*

"Here you are, miss." The driver handed Kristin her light blue valise.

Kristin picked it up and looked once more at the bus. No, he wasn't getting off. He was watching the driver unload the bags. Then he caught Kristin looking at him and, with a start, withdrew further into the bus until she could no longer see him through the tinted glass.

Alexa bent down and tugged at her suitcase. "What an awful hotel! Why don't they have someone here to help us?"

Kristin, her own arms full, said, "Because they don't. Come on, I'll give you a hand in case you start to collapse."

They started up the circular pathway that led to the entrance of the Hotel Daley. It was a big Victorian building that looked every bit of its one hundred or more years, full of turrets and bay windows and setbacks and stained glass windows in unexpected places.

"You sure you'll be all right here, Kristin?" Alexa sounded anxious. "I wish you and your mother could stay with us at the Quadro." Then she stopped. "I'm sorry. I know you can't afford it. I'm a dope."

"It's okay." Kristin looked up at the huge, slightly slanting building they were approaching. "We've never stayed in luxury hotels. Even back in the States, Mother's always choosing something like this — old, slightly decrepit, and . . . cheap."

She grinned. "But she told me Daley's is typically British — very clean and very well run."

She looked up at the old hotel and stopped for a moment, transfixed. It looked like a giant face — two rows of windows on either side of a trellis in the center were like eyes, and a circular doorway at the bottom was a mouth, downturned. It looked like a baleful face — a face of evil.

"Please sign your name on the register," the clerk said in a strange, singsong accent Kristin could not identify.

She signed and looked around.

There were a concierge and a hall porter at a front desk, and from where she stood, a view of a large, musty, high-ceilinged, maroon-carpeted lounge, in which people seated on deep upholstered chairs and sofas were having afternoon tea.

"Wait a sec," Alexa said. "I almost forgot. I have to phone the Quadro to check our reservations."

"Okay. I'll wait here." Kristin watched Alexa start for a bank of phones against the lobby wall.

"Teatime already, Zaram?"

The voice sounded close beside her. Kristin swung her head to see a young man in his early twenties smiling at the desk clerk.

"Yes, Mr. Fayne. Four o'clock." The clerk smiled toothily and turned back to his work.

"Leaving, or just arriving? You're American, aren't you?" The tall young man spoke directly to her.

He had a marked Scottish accent, and his piercing dark brown eyes, leveled at hers, were intense and unnerving.

Kristin, tired and distracted, said, "Excuse me? I didn't — I mean, I don't know . . ." She stopped, feeling foolish.

"Don't know if you're coming or going? Tch, tch. That could be quite confusing." He grinned broadly.

"I didn't mean that," Kristin said sharply. "I'm waiting for my friend, and I haven't even gone to my room yet, and —"

"Please excuse me," the young man said, extending his hand. "I'm Richard Fayne, and I apologize — coming at you like that, asking rude questions."

His brilliant smile flashed again. He pronounced the word *rood*, with a long, musical *oo* sound. Kristin found his accent difficult but charming.

"It's okay. I *am* American. My name is Kristin Mulroy."

He shook her hand. "I'm pleased to know you. Perhaps we could have a spot of tea when you've settled in."

"That would be nice," Kristin said. "Oh, here comes my friend!"

Alexa came up and turned the full power of her blue eyes on the newcomer. As Kristin introduced them, Richard drew a deep breath and said, "I'm *verra* pleased to meet you."

Kristin thought, *Here we go again. I find 'em and she gets 'em.*

Alexa said to Kristin, "Rotten news, Kris. I've

got to go around to the Quadro and claim the room for my folks. And I had a message from my Aunt Betty. I have to get over there by five and have dinner with her. You'll have to eat alone, Kris. Isn't that awful?"

"I don't mind," Kristin said. "But how will you get your bags to the hotel? Take a taxi? Or shall I help you?"

"No problem," Richard Fayne said. "The Quadro is only one square away. A smashing new hotel — one of the best." He picked up Alexa's bag. "This one yours? Och, it's heavy. Come on, I'll take it over to your hotel — then dash back to have tea with you, Kristin. Meet you down here in ten minutes? Right! Let's go."

Kristin nodded, pleased that he was coming back to take her to tea. She followed the porter as he carried her bags to an iron-grilled elevator whose sign said LIFT. He was a short, dark-skinned, black-haired man, who said to her in a strange accent — Indian, Portuguese, Arabic? — "Thees ees fourth floor."

He led the way through a long corridor. The heavy wool carpeting, once luxurious, showed bald patches. The wallpaper, in a small floral pattern so dear to Victorians, was faded and worn.

He opened the door of Room 1107 and brought her bags into a narrow, high-ceilinged room. Despite the pale sun slanting in, it was dreary.

"Here you are, Miss." He handed her the key and she tipped him with a fifty-pence piece (too little? too much?), and he left.

The room was sparsely furnished. A double bed

was tucked in one corner; an ugly chest of drawers and a small dressing table were against the opposite wall; and a tall, oppressive coffin of a wardrobe rose darkly to the ceiling, adding gloom to a room as shabby as the corridor outside.

Was *this* the hotel her mother had been so excited about? Hard to believe. "Charming, perfectly kept, a little jewel of a hotel," her mother had told her. But her mother had last seen it five years before. It certainly had gone to seed in the meantime.

She suddenly felt depressed, then caught sight of her downcast face in the mirror over the bulky chest of drawers and had to laugh at her expression. What she was going to do was get out of there as fast as possible, if not faster, and dash down to meet — what was his name? Oh, yes, Richard Fayne. She wished Alexa didn't have to go to her aunt's house and could spend the night here with her.

She washed up at a little sink in the corner of the room, put on a dab of lip gloss, brushed her hair, and looked again in the small, clouded mirror above the dresser. What she saw was a fairly tall young woman of seventeen with long, light brown hair, even features, and clear brown eyes fringed with black lashes. She made a face at herself in the mirror, then laughed aloud. What was she doing up here when she was about to have her first English tea — and with Richard Fayne? She took a last look around, then hurried out of the room.

After waiting for the old elevator for at least

five minutes, she started to walk down the broad, carpeted staircase. On the way down from the third floor, she passed a man who looked like somebody from the Middle East — Egyptian or Lebanese or Syrian. He seemed familiar, then she realized why — he looked very much like Omar Sharif, the movie actor. He greeted her with dark glowing eyes and a deep-voiced, "Good afternoon," and proceeded up the stairs as she headed downward. *There sure are a lot of friendly people in this hotel.* She smiled happily and descended the final few steps to the lobby.

At the reception desk, she saw him — tall, tweedy, dark-haired. Richard Fayne. He spun about, picked up a small valise, and smiled.

"Ah! I wondered where you were. Sorry, Kristin, but I must leave, at once. Most unexpectedly."

Before she could speak, he thrust a hand forward, and seized her hand. "Too bad, Kristin — perhaps another time."

Kristin managed a, "Well, good-bye," and then he was gone.

She turned to the desk clerk and said, "Please. Do you have any messages for me? Kristin Mulroy?"

"One moment." He moved to the wall behind him where row upon row of pigeonholes were marked alphabetically.

"M — Mulroy — hmm . . ." He reached into the *M* slot and took out a handful of letters and messages. He riffled through them, then said, "Sorry, Miss, nothing here for you."

"My mother said she might be here today. If not, then tomorrow," Kristin said. "I'm supposed to have a message from her."

"There is nothing," the man said. "Perhaps later?"

Disappointed again. First Alexa running off like that — not her fault, of course. Then Richard Fayne running off. Now, no message from her mother.

She felt strangely uneasy. The thought of that annoying airplane steward flashed inexplicably to her mind.

What's wrong with me? This is getting ridiculous. Everything was fine. What she would do now was go into the lounge, have some tea, and relax.

They were riding unevenly along in the small Fiat car. Margaret Clark wondered what her daughter Kristin was doing. She should have arrived in London by now, and with any luck would be registered at Daley's and would have received the telephone message she had left this morning by way of greeting.

I hope I'm doing the right thing, *she thought.*

For the first time, she had her doubts. She stole a look at Pamela, who was paying strict attention to her driving as they neared the little town of Haworth. The road was very narrow and there were few cars out on this cloudy day.

Suppose this trip was, as she had written Kristin, a wild goose chase? All she would have missed was one day with Kristin in London. Besides, Pamela had shown her some papers that certainly looked authentic. What if the Brontës hadn't written their books themselves? Really, it had been too tempting an offer to refuse.

But I mustn't take too long tracking it down. Pamela says the final proof is in Haworth. I'll do a tour of the town and the parsonage as soon as we get there. Then tomorrow I'll make the morning train to London and meet Kristin at Daley's.

She stole another look at the self-possessed, blonde young woman beside her in the car and suddenly felt uneasy.

CHAPTER 2

Kristin walked into the lounge, sat down on a comfortable maroon mohair sofa, and looked about. A small, dark, thin young man in a waiter's uniform, with somewhat ragged cuffs and collar, came over.

"You weesh to order tea, perhaps?" His was definitely an Indian accent. His thin fingers drummed impatiently on an order pad.

"Why, yes," Kristin said, wondering why there was no menu.

As if reading her thoughts, he said, obviously impatient, "No menu, Miss. I bring you some sandwiches, some sweet, some tea? Perhaps you prefer coffee?"

"Fine," she said. "Whatever you think. But tea, please, not coffee."

He muttered something and disappeared behind heavy green draperies in the rear.

"Not very friendly," a strange voice said.

Kristin turned to see the man who looked like Omar Sharif.

"They're rather understaffed here," he said.

"And what staff they do have are mostly students and not very efficient."

Close up, he was extremely handsome, in the classic Egyptian mold.

He indicated the seat beside her and said, "May I?" As Kristin nodded, he extended his hand. "I am Farouk Kalemi. And you?"

"Kristin Mulroy," she said. They shook hands and he sat down.

It was one of the easiest conversations imaginable. Farouk was gracious, worldly, charming, and seemed frankly delighted by Kristin's youth and the fact that she was American.

"America is the most exciting country in the world," he said, looking her over with approving eyes. "And American women are the most fascinating on earth."

Kristin didn't know how to handle this man's extravagant compliments. He didn't seem to be making a pass at her. He was in his early thirties, she guessed; there was a tinge of gray at his temples and crinkly laugh lines at the corners of his eyes.

The Indian waiter returned, wheeling a tea cart. Farouk, seeing Kristin's hesitation, took over. The cart held a teapot and teacups, and a small plate of limp, crustless sandwiches; beside them there was a tired-looking chocolate layer cake.

"This is your first English tea?" Farouk asked. He sounded annoyed.

"Yes," Kristin said. "Is something wrong?"

"Allow me." He turned to the waiter and spoke

rapidly in a foreign tongue. The waiter, flushed, put the teacups down and hastily left. Within minutes, he returned with a loaded tea cart. On the top shelf were several platters of sandwiches — some open-faced, some not, with all kinds of fillings: chicken and cucumber and sardines and ham and watercress and fine English cheese. On a lower shelf, dessert had been miraculously transformed as well. There was a huge bowl of English trifle — slices of cake layered with whipped cream and luscious fruits; a shining silver bowl of creamy chocolate mousse; small chocolate eclairs and napoleons; and a platter of hot, steaming scones with a jug of wild strawberry jam and a dish of yellow butter beside it.

"Now, this is what the English call 'a proper English tea,'" Farouk said. He handled a five-pound note to the waiter, who nodded, pleased.

"It's peculiar, the way people learn to short-change other people," Farouk said, pouring a cup of steaming tea for Kristin. "This spread costs very little more than the first one that chap brought."

"Really?" Kristin said, unbelieving.

"Absolutely," Farouk said. "The beggar is either too lazy to assemble a decent tray or has orders not to serve one to a tourist. Tell me, what are you doing in London? Is this a pleasure trip?"

"Yes," Kristin said, "I'm meeting my mother. She isn't here yet, so she'll probably arrive to-morrow evening. She's been teaching up in Edinburgh the past six weeks, and we're going to tour the British Isles."

"I envy you," Farouk said. "My visit is strictly business. I import antiques to my country, Egypt. I've been here a week; I must return home next week." He sighed. "Ah, if only I could be young and carefree as you are, Kristin."

When they finished their tea, Kristin said, "That was delicious. But why do they call it tea? It's a real meal."

"No, it isn't," Farouk said. "Listen, Kristin, you say your mother is probably not arriving until tomorrow." She nodded. "Then, please, will you have dinner with me tonight? There is a wonderful Italian restaurant in Soho — Luigi's. Won't you join me for dinner?" His dark eyes sought hers.

What have I got to lose? thought Kristin. She wished she could have spent the night with Alexa, but that was out. Farouk was very polite, a gentleman. Her only alternative was to be alone on her first night in London. It seemed too lonely a prospect.

"Thank you, Farouk," she said. "It's very nice of you."

"We'll have a fine time," Farouk promised. He was pleased. "Shall we say eight o'clock?"

"Great. I'll meet you in the lobby."

She took the creaking elevator upstairs and entered her room thoughtfully. In the moment before she flicked on the light, she imagined that a shadow moved on the small balcony outside her window, reflecting on the wall from the waning light outside. But when she snapped on the light, there was nothing.

She felt tired and lay down on the bed to rest. Lying there, alone, she felt uneasy. She wished it were tomorrow. The Bowers would arrive tonight, her mother would be here tomorrow. They'd probably have a meal or go to the theater with Mr. and Mrs. Bower and Alexa. Then on Sunday she and her mother would really start their vacation. She felt a pang of homesickness for her mother. Above all she wondered how and where her mother was.

Margaret Clark stood in the lobby of the Black Bull Inn and waited for Pamela to rejoin her.

The visit to the Brontë parsonage had been very disappointing.

"Just keep this place in mind, Professor Clark," Pamela had said. "Tomorrow, when we visit Top Withens, you'll be able to put the whole history of the family together."

Minutes later, they'd gone to their rooms, washed up, and gone downstairs to dinner in the old inn. The waiter had taken their order for dinner; now they sat at a small table before a roaring fire in the ancient room. The shadows on Pamela Ruthven's face added a certain strangeness to her beauty.

"Are you upset?" Pamela asked. Her eyes probed Margaret Clark's face, concerned.

"No, I'm not. Why should I be?" Margaret coughed. "We're simply investigating a theory, aren't we? If we fail to find proof" —she shrugged — "well, that happens in my field, Pamela. I can't

tell you how many expeditions of this sort have ended in failure."

"Oh, but not this one." Pamela's eyes glowed. "Not this one, Dr. Clark." She seized Margaret's hand on the table and squeezed it. "You'll see! I promise you, you'll see!"

Margaret Clark felt again that little stirring of unhappiness. She had to force herself to relax.

So what if it's been a mistake? *she thought.* I'll go to Top Withens with her first thing in the morning, see what there is to see, and then bid her good-bye. *The ugly thought came that it was possible that the papers, the girl's pursuit of the past, her accusations against the Brontës, were an aberration of Pamela's. It happened all the time with scholars.*

She sighed. She wished she hadn't come. There, she'd finally admitted it to herself. Well, tomorrow morning she'd get the whole thing over with, one way or the other, and say good-bye to Pamela.

She felt relieved. She would phone the Hotel Daley right now, talk to Kristin and tell her she'd definitely be down on the three-thirty train tomorrow. Thank goodness, Kristin was with Alexa, and the Bowers would be arriving later tonight. It was a relief to know that.

It was five minutes to eight. Kristin, wearing a full silk blouse and a slim skirt that hugged her waistline and swirled about her knees gracefully, looked into the mirror. The skirt was lavender; the top matched it exactly, and yet she felt something was missing. She turned to the bureau, took out a broad gold leather belt, and snapped it about her waist. Perfect. Then she added a small pair of gold loop earrings her mother had given her for her seventeenth birthday only a few weeks before. She slipped on a pair of black suede strapped sandals. Now she was ready.

She picked up a small, silver-framed, hinged double picture — one of her, one of her mother — she had bought as a present for her mother last week, and on impulse she put it in her purse. *To keep me company.* She laughed at the silliness of it.

She was about to turn out the light when she stopped and looked toward the balcony. Funny, she had the strangest feeling that someone was watching her. *There's no one there*, she reassured herself, and stepped out into the corridor.

From the terrace, a shadowy figure watched the young American girl close the door behind her.

"Did you have a good time?" Farouk asked as they entered the lobby of the Hotel Daley. It was twelve o'clock.

"It was marvelous. I really loved it." Kristin meant every word.

Farouk was an enchanting companion. He had kept her entertained with anecdotes about his home in Egypt, his childhood, his adventures since leaving home. And in between, he had an endless string of amusing stories, some of the funniest jokes she'd ever heard in her life. She tried hard to remember some of them to tell Alexa.

It was a pleasant night and they could have continued talking and laughing, but suddenly Kristin felt tired.

"Of course," Farouk said. "It's jet lag that you are beginning to feel. It comes over one all at once."

He took her to her door and said lightly, "I'll see you tomorrow, Kristin. It has been a very pleasant evening." He turned and left her.

She fumbled with her key and had a little difficulty getting it into the lock. Then it worked, and she opened the door and snapped on the light.

A scene of devastation met her eyes. Drawers had been ripped open, closet doors flung wide; even the bedding had been torn from the bed and left in utter confusion. She was terribly, terribly frightened. She looked across the room and thought she saw a huge black shadow on the balcony. She muffled a scream and raced out of the room. She didn't wait for the elevator but sped down the stairs.

Breathless, she arrived at the reception desk. The young Indian clerk looked at her in surprise.

"There is something wrong, Madam?" he asked.

"There certainly is," she said agitatedly. "Someone broke into my room! It's a wreck!"

She saw the clerk's knowing glance at his companion behind the desk, as if to say, "She's crazy." Then he turned back to her. "Surely you are mistaken," he said with amusement.

"No! Come and see," she said urgently. "It's terrible!"

Reluctantly, he followed her to the elevator. They ascended to the fourth floor.

"Yes, I see." He looked at the room, then back at her skeptically. "It would appear that someone has been looking for something. Is anything missing?"

His singsong speech made light of her predicament.

"I don't know. Wait here while I take a look," she said nervously.

He glanced at his watch and clucked. "I do not have time to stand here. Check your belongings, please." He clucked again. "I shall be at the desk downstairs."

"No! You can't leave me like this!" Kristin said angrily. "I'm afraid. Someone broke into this room. I don't want to be alone here."

He crossed swiftly to the window and looked outside on the balcony. "My dear young woman. There is no one there." He locked the wooden shutters. "There, you see? Closed. Tight. No one can come in, I promise you. No one."

Even as she protested, he left.

Alone, Kristin conquered her fear enough to make a hasty check of the bureau drawers, her suitcase, the closet. As far as she could tell, nothing was missing.

She walked downstairs again, depressed. The

clock above the desk said 12:25. Too late to call Alexa or the Bowers. She was dead with exhaustion, and Alexa and her family must be, too — probably sound asleep by now.

The clerk with the singsong accent said, "Yesss??? You learned what is missing?" His voice seemed to be mocking her.

"No. I don't know if anything was taken. But why would anyone do such a thing?" She fought to keep hysteria out of her voice. "Please help me!"

"Nothing I can do, I'm afraid," the clerk said. "You understand, I am alone now. All night." He pondered a minute. "Perhaps it was just a prank. I have already asked the night maid to tidy up your room." With a polite little nod, he turned away.

There was nothing more she could do. She would have to wait until morning.

Upstairs, alone in the room, which had been superficially set in order by the maid, she felt unhappy and anxious. She would call Farouk first thing in the morning. She lay awake in the dark a long time before dropping off into a troubled sleep.

"I'm sorry," the clerk said the next day, "but Mr. Kalemi has left already — for good."

"You must be making a mistake. He told me he would be here another week at least," Kristin said.

"I'm sorry," the clerk repeated. "Mr. Kalemi checked out at seven-thirty this morning."

That's strange, Kristin thought. *Why would he go away without even saying good-bye?*

Did he have something to do with what happened to my room?

CHAPTER 3

The meal was everything Kristin had ever been led to expect of an English breakfast: rashers of fabulous cured country ham; eggs bubbling in butter; kippers, fried with onions and absolutely delicious; stacks of hot buttered toast with jars of wild strawberry jam and jugs of orange marmalade; fried browned potatoes with bacon bits; and silver pots of steaming coffee, tea, and cocoa.

She ate much more than she'd intended and felt considerably better when she left the dining room. Maybe the hotel was staffed with foreigners from nations on different continents, but they certainly had learned the English way of doing breakfast.

Kristin walked into the lobby, looking for a phone where she could call Alexa and still have some privacy. She was wondering if she should walk to the Hotel Quadro when she heard a yell.

"Kristin!"

Kristin ran to Alexa and hugged her.

"Alexa! Wait till I tell you what's happened! You'll never believe it!"

She dragged Alexa into the lounge, unoccupied at this early hour, and they sat down on a sofa.

Alexa looked lovely. She was a slim, well-made brunette with mischievous blue-gray eyes and dark hair, chicly dressed in beige pants; her dazzling orange-and-white striped tunic contrasted marvelously with her coloring.

"Shoot!" she said. "I can't wait!"

Kristin told her everything, from the moment she'd had tea with Farouk to the delightful dinner they'd had in Soho, and then finished with the news of the break-in.

"Come on!" Alexa's blue eyes widened. "You're *sure* you're not exaggerating?"

"Are you crazy? Everything I own was thrown around the room like a cyclone had struck! Why would I make up such a story?" Kristin sounded hurt.

"Who do you think did it? Robbers — looking for jewels?" Alexa asked.

"*My* jewels? Don't be dumb, Alexa. Anyone can see I'm just a teenage tourist." Kristin stopped. "Oh! You mean — why would anyone want to wreck *my* room and search *my* things?"

"Because they had the wrong room," Alexa said. "I'll bet that's what it is. Maybe they wanted to get into someone else's room. Like that Farouk guy. He's a rich importer, right?"

"That's a possibility," Kristin conceded. "His room was only two doors away from mine."

"You know," Alexa said, "there's one thing that I don't get."

"What's that?"

"If he's such a rich businessman, what's he doing in a dump like the Daley? He ought to be in the Dorchester or the Quadro — someplace like that," Alexa finished logically.

"You're right. It doesn't add up." Kristin sighed. "Thank goodness, my mother will be here today. I can't wait to check out of here."

"Mother and Dad are waiting for us back at the hotel. Come on, we'll have some fun for a change."

Alexa and Kristin walked quickly along two or three streets of houses with carefully kept lawns and small, colorful gardens until they came to a large, imposing building, extremely modern in design. A huge blinking sign, QUADRO, ran across the rooftop.

Margaret Clark felt better now that she had made the second phone call. She had missed Kristin both times, but left word that she would arrive at seven tonight. That meant she had to make the three-thirty train from Leeds.

She shivered and pulled her coat closer about her. It was a bleak, windy day in Yorkshire. The cold penetrated the little car as it made its way along the narrow road leading out of town.

Margaret wished she hadn't promised to visit the moors. "But it's the original site of Wuthering Heights," *Pamela had said with authority. Margaret wondered now exactly how much of Pamela's theory and research was authentic and how much — she hated even to think it — was embroidery to fit her theory.*

"This is the last lap of our journey." Pamela turned the car off the little highway onto a narrow dirt road. "We'll be there in just a few moments. Are you comfortable?"

"Yes. I'm fine." Dr Clark tried to keep her impatience out of her voice. I wish we could turn around right now, *she thought, irritated.* What am I doing here?

The little car climbed the small dirt road as a light rain began to fall. By the time they reached the top of the hill, the few tourists who had been strolling there were making their way downhill, some on foot, some by car.

She was about to ask Pamela if they should go on, when the young blonde woman pulled the car to a halt beside a low stone wall that marked the beginning of the moors.

"Why are we stopping here?" Margaret Clark asked.

"Can't go any further, not by car, anyway," Pamela replied. "The house is right over there." She pointed to a dark gray building higher up the moor. She flung the car door open and said, "You can use the umbrella. I like the feel of the rain and the wind." She gave a little laugh.

Dr. Clark thought, Oh well, having gone this far, I've got to be patient enough to see it through.

She smiled back at Pamela, opened the umbrella, and followed her up the dirt path. As she walked behind the girl, she looked far off in the distance and saw a vague gray mass of stone that was Top Withens.

* * *

Alexa's mother was an older version of her daughter — sleek, pretty, blue-eyed, and charming. Mr. Bower, a tall, distinguished man, was obviously an affluent American. Both greeted Kristin warmly.

"Your mother is due today?" Mrs. Bower asked. "When?"

"I wish I could be sure," Kristin said, frowning. "She was supposed to phone if she was making the three-thirty from Leeds, but she hasn't."

"Don't worry, Kristin," Mr. Bower said. "She knows that you've been with Alexa and that we're here, too. She's probably hurrying down to London now, too busy to stop to phone."

"Wait till you hear what's been happening!" Alexa said. "It's ghastly! Tell them, Kris."

"Not here," Mrs. Bower said. "Let's go up to our suite."

As they crossed the lobby, Kristin saw that the Hotel Quadro was as far removed from the Hotel Daley as any place on earth could be. The lobby was huge — orange with brown and chrome and glass accents, a mélange of hard crystal and other unyielding materials that were uninviting but efficient and striking.

Mr. Bower took Kristin's news calmly. "I wouldn't worry, Kristin," he said. "I agree with Alexa — it was a mistake. A question of the wrong room. No one would want to burglarize either you or your mother, I'm sure. What they want is rich tourists — though I doubt there are any at Daley's."

"Don't give it another thought." Mrs. Bower patted Kristin on the head. "There are several good reasons why you're upset. One, it's your first trip to Europe; two, it must be terrible to find your room left in such awful shape; and three — now what was three . . . ?" She broke off, looking vague. Mrs. Bower had a way of forgetting her thread of thought. Far from being stupid, she was simply a woman with an active mind who didn't focus for very long on anything, a trait which endeared her to her husband.

"Stella, there you go." Mr. Bower obviously enjoyed his wife's confusion. "Can't you concentrate at all?" He turned to Kristin. "Can you imagine my wife in my position on the Exchange?"

He was a stockbroker in Chicago who made a great deal of money trading — buying and selling wheat and other commodities. "They rattle the prices off a mile a minute. You've got to be quick and able to remember every little detail if you expect to last down there, I tell you." He smiled again at his wife. "Good thing I love you, Stella."

It made Kristin uncomfortable whenever Mr. Bower treated his wife like that, as if she were a child or had some kind of handicap. Still, Mrs. Bower did nothing to change his attitude. *I guess they like it that way*, she was thinking as Mrs. Bower suddenly clapped her forehead.

"Oh, I know! I know what the third thing is, Kristin! It's your mother. She'll be here soon and we'll all be together, at least for tonight, and then you can start your vacation with her tomorrow, while we spend the week here in London." She looked at her husband. "Herbert has business, very important business, to transact in England."

She beamed at her husband, and he straightened his shoulders and smiled at her. *That* is *the way they like it*, Kristin thought. But it made her uneasy all the same.

"I'll tell you what," Mr. Bower said to Alexa. "Why don't you take Kristin to your room, show her all the gadgets, then meet us back here. We'll check the Hotel Daley once more for messages on our way to the museum."

"But, Charles, Kristin is expecting her mother," Mrs. Bower said anxiously. "She probably wants to wait at the hotel for her."

"Nonsense," Mr. Bower said. "Wait for the kettle to boil? Doesn't make sense, Stella." He turned to Kristin. "You'll come with us, Kristin?"

"Yes. Yes, I will," Kristin said, privately preferring to stay. On the other hand, her mother had written that she'd most likely be arriving that evening at seven. If she had changed her plans, she would have let Kristin know.

"Wait until you see all the gimmicks in this room," Alexa said. "You'll faint."

Alexa's room was fairly small but very attractive. "It's a bedsitter — a combination bedroom and living room," she explained. "Very big over here — I guess because it's such a small island and there are so many people.

"Now get this!" She pointed to a huge cabinet low along one wall. On its front there were ten or twelve buttons with small rectangular lights, labeled GIN, SCOTCH, several other kinds of liquor, as well as SODA WATER, COKE, PEANUTS, GRAPE DRINK, CHOCOLATES, PRETZELS.

"All you do is push a button." Alexa demonstrated, pressing the one marked PEANUTS. There was a *whirr* and a small panel in the cabinet opened, revealing a bag of roasted peanuts.

"Wonderful!" Kristin cupped her hand as Alexa ripped the bag open and poured out some nuts.

"That's not all," Alexa said. "Would you believe this machine not only serves you but automatically — by computer — rings up the charge, which goes right to the bookkeeping department? When you check out, it's all on your bill."

"Sensational," Kristin said. "A robot servant."

"Right. Now look . . ." Alexa said, opening a large panel in the cabinet. "See this? There are rolls, juice, milk, coffee, tea, whatever you want, courtesy of the hotel, no charge. "A breakfast, waiting when you wake up —" She broke off. "Huh, that's funny."

"What is?" Kristin came over to her side.

"This." Alexa indicated a cigarette on the metal food cabinet. It had been smoked halfway, then placed on the cabinet, where it had burned a long scar into the surface.

"Isn't that your father's?" Kristin asked.

"My dad stopped smoking. Didn't you notice? He hates it now." Alexa picked up the cigarette and looked at the imprint. "Saharas. An Egyptian cigarette." She turned to Kristin. "Who could have put that there?"

"Anyone," Kristin said. "A porter, a maid, someone who came in to clean the windows or fix something."

"They don't do that here," Alexa said. "My father said that's the good thing about this hotel. Nobody comes in your room, ever, for any reason, unless they have your permission. There've been too many robberies."

She was about to drop the cigarette butt in a wastebasket when she noticed something else.

"How about this, Kristin?" She pointed to a half-open bureau drawer. "I didn't leave that drawer like that!"

"How do you know you didn't?"

"Because I turned back as I was leaving to see that everything in the room was neat. I saw that same drawer open, and I closed it." She said firmly, "It's got my diary in it, that's why I did it."

They looked at each other in silence.

"Someone's been looking through my things," Alexa said.

"I know what you're thinking." Kristin looked thoughtful. "Maybe it's the same one who broke into my room and messed it up. Right?"

"Right." Alexa, frustrated, banged her fist on the bureau. "Let's go down and tell my parents."

Mr. Bower refused to take the matter seriously. "What in the world would anyone want with your room, Alexa? A crook would have broken into *our* room."

"But the same thing happened to Kristin," Alexa protested.

"Coincidence. Not important."

He took his wife's arm and said to the girls, "Follow me. I'm the leader."

They followed, with Kristin thinking, *I only hope he knows what he's doing.*

"Are you sure there's been no word for Miss Mulroy? Her mother was to have phoned her," Mr. Bower said.

The dark young man at the desk shuffled some papers nervously.

"No, no. I have tell her before. No one leave message. You see?" He pulled open a drawer. There were envelopes and stamps and some postcards in it. He took out a small box with telephone message slips in it. "Anderson, Kalaki, Petrov . . ." He read off all the names. "They will soon arrive. That is why slips are in drawer. If she, Miss Kristin Mulroy, have message from mother, it is here in drawer or there"— he pointed to the nest of cubbyholes in the wall —"in compartment for Room 1107." He put his hand in the empty space, drew it out, and said dramatically, "She has nothing. Nothing!"

"No need to get excited," Mr. Bower said. He withdrew a bill from his wallet. "Please be sure, if a message comes, to see that Miss Mulroy gets it. Understood?"

"Understood," said the clerk, pocketing the bill. Too bad the girl was upset, but what difference did it make, anyway? Her mother would show up sometime that night and that was all that mattered.

"You really shouldn't worry, dear," Mrs. Bower

said as they left the lobby. "Your mother is on her way to London. She'll be here by evening."

"You know my mother," Kristin said. "She would never keep me guessing like this, when all it takes is one phone call. It isn't like her. She'd have wanted to know if I arrived safely. She'd want me to know when she'd be here."

"I guess you've checked the train schedule," Mr. Bower said. "When is the last train tonight? Seven o'clock?"

"Yes," Kristin said quietly.

"Then let's not worry one more moment about it, Kristin. We're off to the British Museum, then we're taking you to high tea at our hotel, and then we're off to the station to meet your mother. Got that?"

Kristin responded to Mr. Bower's taking charge. As they rode in the taxi to the British Museum, she sat back and made herself relax. Her mother would arrive tonight, and that would be the end of her worries.

As Margaret Clark followed Pamela across the moors, there was a brisk wind whipping around them. Several small clusters of tourists, with cameras and tote bags, passed them coming from the opposite direction. In the distance, black sheep were grazing on the bright green clumps of grass, brushing against the peat-black soil. The sheep, the soil, the gray-black cobblestone fence, seemed painted with the same brush, blending into each other, hewn out of the ancient moors.

Abruptly, the stone fence ended. Ahead there

was a steeply descending hill; the moor broke suddenly to a dark gully where water rushed down with great force over a sharp stone ledge. The path they were on had become damp, then wet, then muddy. A man and a woman coming up from the waterfall stopped to speak to them.

"Better be careful from 'ere on in," the man said. "It's easy to lose your footing."

"If I was you," the woman said, "I wouldn't go in there at all."

"Oh?" Margaret said.

"Look 'ere." The woman indicated the side of her skirt, which was heavily daubed with thick mud. "If it 'adn't been for me 'usband, I'd 'ave like to broke me neck."

"Thank you," Margaret Clark said. "It's nice of you to warn us."

Pamela said nothing. She gave them a curt nod and moved off. Margaret Clark was annoyed. More than annoyed. She did not want to go any further. A slight rain had begun to fall from the dark clouds massed overhead. The wind was stronger now. How had she come to be in such a fantastic situation? Out in this cold, friendless, deserted place with this strange young woman who had managed somehow to convince her of what she now knew was a baseless story. She wanted to speak to Pamela, but the young woman was speeding on now and it was increasingly difficult to keep up with her.

"Pamela! Pamela, stop!" she shouted.

Pamela turned around. Her face was in the shadows in the dark gully. "Yes?"

"I want to speak with you," Margaret said sharply. She stood her ground and waited till Pamela came closer. Margaret was terribly aware of their isolation. The rain was coming down hard; it had driven the last tourist from the moor. There was no one there, nothing. Even the sheep were gone. A lone goat bleated its way into the brush and disappeared. The only sound was the roar of the waterfall fifty yards below.

Margaret had to raise her voice to make herself heard.

"This is a mistake," she said.

Pamela's eyes glittered coldly. "A mistake?"

Margaret held her hand out palm upward. "Yes," she said. "We can just make it back to the car now if we hurry."

Pamela said nothing. She just stood there looking at her with a stone-cold face, her dark shiny eyes never leaving Margaret's, holding her fixed. Margaret shuddered and said, firmly, "I'm going back now. I think we should both go back."

Pamela stared at her. "I don't think so," she said tonelessly.

"I don't know what you have in mind, Pamela. But this has gone quite far enough. I'm leaving." She turned and started back along the path.

"Professor Clark! Wait up!" the blonde woman shouted.

Margaret turned to see Pamela standing there, her fists clenched, her face a mask.

"Don't go any farther, Professor Clark," Pamela said harshly. "You'll regret it if you do."

She's mad, *Margaret thought. Without a word,*

Margaret turned back and hurried down the thick mud path. The woman is out of her mind, trying to frighten me this way. *This was a nightmare scene from a horror movie. It couldn't be happening to her.*

Behind her she heard the squush *of footsteps hurrying, then she felt a tug on her arm.*

Margaret looked desperately over the moorland. There was no one. No one to help. She swung about with unusual vigor to face her adversary — and lost her balance. Her right leg slid awkwardly out from under her, and as she fell she heard an ominous snap!

"Oh, my God," she said, as the pain began, "I've broken my leg!"

CHAPTER 4

They wandered through the huge halls of the British Museum and were spellbound by the sights.

"I can't believe it." Alexa managed to keep her voice down. "It's the real, actual, honest to goodness, original, one and only Magna Carta! Do you believe it?"

It was strong stuff. Kristin, looking at the ancient manuscript in the glass case, felt a thrill as she realized that a hand had held the pen above this parchment scroll in the year 1215 A.D. — more than seven hundred years ago.

"It's mind-boggling, Alexa. King John himself signed it!" A chill swept through her, leaving goose bumps on her arm.

"It's to die from, Kristin." Alexa's eyes were wide.

"Where's your British accent?" Kristin asked innocently.

Mr. Bower came up to them. "Feeling better now, Kristin? This really takes your mind off your worries, doesn't it?"

"I'm so glad you took us here, Mr. Bower. It does give a feeling that life goes on and on, no matter what."

He was pleased. "Good girl. Just remember that. Everything works out for the best."

But as he walked away to rejoin his wife, Kristin thought, *Why, that's what Pangloss said in Voltaire's* Candide, *and was he ever wrong!* No matter how horrible the things were that happened to him and to his master, Candide, Pangloss simply said, "In this best of all possible worlds . . . all is for the best."

She smiled. *I'll talk to Mother about that tonight. She has a more philosophical mind than Mr. Bower. She's smarter, too. She's just not as bossy as he is.*

Feeling like a traitor thinking those thoughts, she hurried her steps and followed Alexa, who was trailing after her parents.

She could hardly wait. What was it? Another four hours till her mother arrived.

Victoria Station was crowded. The big clock, high over their heads in the glass-domed, sprawling, ancient train station, said 6:45.

Kristin and Alexa pushed their way through the throngs of people coming and going, cutting across their path, sometimes blocking it completely.

"This way!" Alexa shouted as she found an opening in the milling mob. "Follow me!"

Kristin felt guilty as she elbowed an Englishman out of the way. The English were so polite, they were always a little surprised whenever Alexa or she walked aggressively ahead, through, or around them.

"Platform 31." The trains were heaving their way into the station. A smoky haze peppered with soot overhung the platforms, from which people were emerging.

Kristin felt good inside. All these people arriving.

Her mother would be coming up the ramp of Platform 31 in just a moment. Kristin eagerly searched the faces of the people pouring through the gate. Every moment or so, someone in the crowd of arrivals would recognize a waiting figure and there was a cry of welcome and a hug. Kristin felt a pang of longing as she saw others embracing.

Where *was* her mother? She and Alexa, who was waiting at the opposite side of the gate, exchanged glances. Alexa said, "She'll be here in a minute! Take it easy!"

But a minute passed, another, and another. The thick line of people narrowed down to a single file, and then there were just stragglers.

"I'm going down to the train," Kristin said, and started down the ramp to where the train steamed on the tracks.

"Here, miss! You can't do that!" A ruddy-faced trainman called angrily after Kristin, but Alexa hurried up to him.

"Excuse me," she said, "can you tell me if this is the three-thirty from Leeds?"

"Yes, Miss, it is indeed." He stared at her

closely. "And I gave you that information not five minutes ago."

She pulled at his jacket. "Please, I have to know. Is there a later train tonight?"

"There is not." He glared at her clutching hand and she let go of his sleeve. "Is there a problem?"

"There may be," Alexa said. She pointed toward the train platform, where Kristin was looking in the train windows for any remaining passengers.

"That your friend?" The conductor was more kindly. "American, aren't you?"

"Yes. And I think — I'm practically sure — her mother didn't make it down to London."

"Pity. But then there's another train tomorrow." He watched as Kristin started back up the ramp. "Happens all the time. Someone misses a train. Fact of life, young lady."

Kristin was walking dispiritedly up the ramp, alone, not a passenger in sight.

"She does look a bit down, doesn't she?" the man whispered.

"There's been no word from her mother for two days," Alexa said.

"Is that a fact now?" the man said, impressed.

"Yes," Alexa said sadly. "Her mother would never do that. Something must have happened to her."

"You're sure of that?" Mr. Bower said into the phone. "She left four days ago? Wednesday — you're sure? I see." He hung up the phone and said to the others, "That confirms it. Margaret left the university in Edinburgh Wednesday afternoon. The housemother said she's pretty sure she left in a car with someone — she thinks a blonde woman. But she didn't know who it was."

They were gathered in the bright, shiny Quadro lounge — Alexa, her parents, and Kristin. On a low table before them was a platter of small dessert cakes, and beside it the usual teapot and cups. The orange plastic phone, on a long cord, was being removed by a waiter.

"Wednesday afternoon?" Kristin repeated. "How long does it take to drive from Edinburgh to London?"

"That's not the point," Mr. Bower said. "Your mother mentioned a trip in her letter. She probably planned to visit Loch Lomond, or one of the other lakes. They're a great tourist attraction."

"I don't think my mother just went off sightseeing. You're all trying to make everything sound normal." Kristin's voice rose. "And it isn't! It isn't normal! My mother is in trouble somewhere. We've got to *do* something! Go to the police —"

"All right," Mr. Bowers said. "If we don't hear from her by tomorrow morning, we'll go right to the police. That's a promise, Kristin." At Kristin's questioning look, he added, "There's very little they can do at this hour of the night to get an investigation going."

"Would you like to stay here with us, Kristin?" Mrs. Bower asked. "Then you and Alexa could be together."

Kristin, pale, said, "I'd rather stay at Daley's.

I want to be right there when my mother comes.'
She gulped, thinking, *If she comes.*

Alexa said, "Mother, can I — ?" just as Mrs. Bower said, "Why don't you sleep at the Daley tonight?" They smiled.

Kristin's eyes filled. The Bowers kissed them good night and the two girls left.

A half hour later, Alexa and Kristin were undressing in Room 1107 at the Daley. Alexa watched Kristin brush her hair listlessly in front of the stained mirror above the bureau. Kristin's face was expressionless, her eyes focused on something far off.

"Stop it, Kristin! I can't stand to see you like this!" Alexa went over to her friend, pulled the brush away from her hair, and stared directly at her.

Kristin tried to break away, but Alexa held her firmly, fingers dug into her arm.

"Speak to me, Kristin! I'm your best friend in the world, right?"

"Alexa, give me a break, please. I don't want to talk —"

"You've got to. How can I let you go to sleep like this? Your head's full of the crazies. Let's talk."

"I'm not crazy. My mother is missing. She's hurt, or . . . or . . ." Her lips quivered.

"She's not dead. That's what you're thinking, isn't it?" Kristin nodded. "If something that bad happened to your mother, we'd know it somehow. She's an American, traveling in England. She's got identification," Alexa said reasonably enough. "Someone would have gotten word to you at the hotel by now."

"All right. I admit that makes sense," Kristin said. "But something has happened. Even you think so."

"Whatever it is, it's for the police to work on. Not us." Alexa turned back the coverlet on the bed. "Go to sleep, Kristin. Think good thoughts. Let's concentrate, both of us. We won't *let* any harm come to your mother."

Kristin said, "Thanks, Alexa. I know you mean well, but tomorrow — *tomorrow* — nothing, no one, can stop me. I'm going to go look for my mother!"

"We'll do what we can, Mr. Bower," the police inspector said. "But there is very little we *can* do at this moment."

In a musty room of the Knightsbridge police station, Alexa felt Kristin tense up beside her.

"May I ask why?" Mr. Bower asked politely.

The inspector, a friendly middle-aged man with a tired air of boredom, said courteously, "Because, sir, this sort of thing happens with tourists practically every day." He held up the letter Margaret Clark had written to Kristin from Edinburgh. "The professor's all charged up about this little expedition she had in mind. You'll grant that?"

"Margaret Clark would never leave her daughter up in the air like this," Mrs. Bower interposed.

"I understand," the inspector said, still politely. "But she does seem to have gone off on some sort of hunt, if you take my meaning. And, in my humble opinion, she's overstayed herself a bit. England is simply not a country where tourists get kidnapped or hijacked — like in some of those foreign places. We've got our faults, we have, but we're a bit more civilized than that." He chuckled. "I'll wager she shows up today, this very evening. Tomorrow morning at the latest, all apologies."

"And if she doesn't?" Mr. Bower said.

"Then come and see me and we'll put out a search order." The inspector stood up from behind his desk, in obvious dismissal.

Outside, they stood on the Brompton Road, which was practically empty this early Sunday morning.

"Now what?" Kristin asked anxiously.

"Well, dear," Mrs. Bower said placatingly, "there seems to be nothing we can do until tomorrow. The inspector said —"

"I don't care what he said," Kristin cut in. "I thought about it all night. I know what I'm going to do. I'm going up to Edinburgh." It sounded rude, but she couldn't help herself.

"Oh, dear," Mrs. Bower said. "Don't be hasty, Kristin. This isn't America. It isn't safe to go traipsing off all alone —"

"Mother," Alexa said warningly. "Kristin means this. She feels she's got to *do* something."

Kristin looked gratefully at her, then spoke to the Bowers. "I'll go crazy just hanging around here, waiting for something to happen. All I want to do is go to the university and talk to the people there in person. I'll find out who saw her last, who saw her leave, look at the place she stayed. That's all."

Mr. Bower took over. "How would you like Alexa to go with you? Is that what you want?"

"Oh, could she?" Kristin was near tears again. She flung her arms around him and held tight.

"Oh, Charles, you've solved the problem, as usual," Mrs. Bower said. She patted Kristin's shoulder. "You've been under an awful strain, you poor girl."

Kristin straightened up and wiped her eyes with the back of her hand. "I don't know what I would have done if it weren't for you and Mr. Bower." She reached to grab Alexa's hand. No need for her to say anything there.

"I guess we should start packing," Alexa said briskly. "There must be a train to Scotland sometime soon."

"Not quite," Mr. Bower smiled. "It's not America, you know. These are smaller countries. There are only two trains a day going as far as Scotland." He took a timetable out of his coat pocket. "There's one leaving at one-thirty, arriving Edinburgh at five-fifteen. Think you can make it?"

Alexa and Kristin exchanged glances. "You bet we can," Alexa said. "Oh, Kristin! Everything's going to be all right. I know it!"

Kristin nodded and they took the elevator up to

Alexa's room, so that she could pack a bag. In her heart, Kristin felt dread foreboding. She had no sense at all that her mother was up there in Edinburgh. For all she knew, her mother might even be dead.

CHAPTER 5

The taxicab driver let them off at the university. It was a huge graystone complex of buildings not unlike a castle itself. They saw it as they rode down Princes Street.

What a beautiful city Edinburgh was! No wonder it was called the "Athens of the North"—with the castle mounted high on the hill overlooking the main street of the city, its broad greensward sweeping down to the beautiful, vivid gardens at the foot of the slope.

"I've never seen anything as beautiful as this in my whole life," Alexa said. "Who would ever think of laying out a city like this?"

"The people that Robert Bruce came from," Kristin said. "The Scots are wild, exciting, poetic."

The cabdriver turned around and beamed at Kristin. "You're a rare young lady. It's a pleasure to hack you."

"Hack? Like Jack the Ripper?" Alexa whispered to Kristin.

The driver let them off at the university. Together they went up the rather steep stone steps and through the heavy black oak doors to the reception desk. There was no one there. They looked around wonderingly.

"May I help you?" It was a young man of about twenty with a gentle Scottish accent.

When they told him what they were after, he said, "I doubt anyone is here to help you, to give you the information you want. The school's pretty well shut down on holiday right now." He sounded truly sorry.

Kristin resigned herself. She could be patient, she could wait until tomorrow morning. What else was there to do?

"Can you suggest someplace where we might stay tonight?"

"You mean you don't have a reservation?" He whistled. "That's bad — this time of year. Even with the festival ended, folks like to stay on. Especially young folk." He hesitated. "I rather favor the Pink Heather myself. If you like, I can ring them for you."

"That would be wonderful, if you don't mind," Kristin said.

"Better than wonderful," Alexa purred. "I'm dead on my feet."

The young man smiled and left them, returning minutes later with the good news.

"By some miracle, they've got a room. Not very grand, but then that makes it cheaper."

They thanked him until he blushed with pleasure, then made their way down the steep steps toward a waiting taxi that looked astonishingly like the one they'd ridden in on the way to the university.

It *was* the same cab, the same driver, beaming anew at serving them again.

"Thought I'd wait a bit to pick up another fare. I'd no idea 'twould be you two young ladies. Hop in!"

He pointed out the few landmarks they were passing on the way. "Bruce's last stand," he said proudly, indicating a tall cypress tree with a small dog bounding ecstatically nearby. "And here's where you get the best haggis in Edinburgh! And this is the jailhouse where Mary Queen of Scots lived," he announced proudly. "Not very long, I must say."

They really were impressed as they rode along the main street, turning right down a tree-lined avenue toward a block of wooden-frame buildings, quite Victorian, with porches ringing them and small, perfect grass and garden plots in front.

"Pink Heather Inn!" the cabman announced, and ran around to open the door for them. When he saw their generous tip, he said, "No need for this, my dears," but they insisted. He tipped his hat and, grinning broadly, left.

The Pink Heather was a huge old house three stories high, with a wide porch in front. A young girl in a maid's uniform opened the glass-windowed front door and took them upstairs to a third-floor bedroom. It was very small, but it had a double bed with a thick feather quilt atop it. One dresser and two chairs completed the furnishings.

"It's the cleanest place I've ever seen," Alexa said.

"There'll be a bit of a do down in the TV room tonight, I'm afraid," the maid said. "It's a bunch of students having a farewell party before they break up for intersession. I hope you'll not be minding the commotion."

As they unpacked Alexa said, "Maybe we'll get a chance to look in on the party." Then she saw Kristin's eyes. "I'm sorry, Kris, I wasn't thinking. I know this isn't a pleasure trip," she added, which made it only worse.

"It's okay," Kristin said, emptying her overnight bag. "Really it is. I'm sorry I'm such a drag."

In that moment they heard a wild yell from downstairs. It could've meant anything, that sound — joy, terror, or pain. They looked at each other and Kristin said, "Let's get out of here."

Alexa said softly, "You're really down, aren't you?"

Tears welled in Kristin's eyes. "I'm scared to death, Alexa. *Where's my mother?* That's all I can think about."

"Now that we're here, we'll find out!" Alexa seized Kristin by the hand and spun her to the door. "Come on! We can't do anything tonight. Let's have dinner and try to have some fun!"

Kristin smiled wanly but followed Alexa down to the second landing. A door was flung open and a young couple looked at them curiously. They were obviously in their late teens, laughing and flushed with the excitement of the party inside.

"What have we here?" the young man said,

with an unmistakable Scottish burr. "Two wanderers from a foreign land, upon my soul."

The girl nodded her head. "Faith, and that they are." She dropped a small curtsy. "We bid you enter, my ladies. 'Tis a great celebration — End of Term!"

Kristin and Alexa were enchanted. The young man bowed low, motioned to the music and clatter from inside, and said, "Prithee, won't you join our merrymaking?"

Alexa nudged Kristin and said, "Prithee and why not? 'Tis a gracious offer indeed! Say you not so, my friend?"

"So say I also," Kristin said. "Lead on, Macduff. 'And damned be him that first cries Hold, enough!"

The Scottish couple broke up and said, "Americans!" in unison, as if they had found a gold mine. The young man stuck out his hand. "I'm Douglas, and she's Joan."

"Alexa, and Kristin," Alexa said. "We were on our way out to dinner."

"We've loads of stuff to eat," Joan said.

"And drink," Douglas added.

He led them into the huge room.

"People! Look what we've found. Two dazzling American beauties. One is Kristin, one's Alexa. I forget which is which," Douglas said.

"A fat lot you forget," Joan said. "The dark one is Alexa, the light-haired one's Kristin." She took a tall young man by the hand. "Edward, introduce the girls to everyone." Then she turned to a slim young woman and said, "Caitlin, be a dear and fetch two plates of food for our friends."

Within minutes Alexa and Kristin were part of the party. Even Kristin began to relax.

At one point a lovely-looking blonde, somewhat older than the rest of the young women — and very flamboyant — got up, seized Douglas by the hand, and began to dance a graceful tango.

"Isn't she sensational?" Alexa said. "Such passion. Like a Spaniard, even though she's obviously Anglo-Saxon." She broke off and said, "What are you staring at? You're not listening."

"Her beads," Kristin said. "That necklace — have you ever seen anything like it?"

Alexa looked. The stones were the size of large pebbles but shot through with the most dazzling colors of the spectrum — yellow, red, orange, blue, green, turquoise — each stone a total blaze of color. The blonde young woman had brownish eyes, whose color seemed to change with each flash of the necklace as it spun about her neck while she dipped and swayed to the guitar music. Some of the people started to sing and clap hands and move with the music as the girl whirled and dipped in the dance, her wide circular skirt flowing gracefully with her every motion.

Neither Kristin nor Alexa noticed the door open; someone joined the cluster of young people in the small anteroom outside their own. All of a sudden the blonde girl stopped the dance in midstep. Snatching up her cape from a nearby sofa, she hurried out of the room in the opposite direction from where Kristin and Alexa stood with the others, surprised at this unexpected development.

"Hey! Where are you going?" exclaimed the tall Scotsman with whom she had been dancing. "You can't leave me like this! I feel a fool, Pamela!"

The blonde paid no attention as she slammed out of the room. It was most peculiar.

"Now, what was that all about?" Alexa whispered to Kristin.

As if in answer to Alexa's question, the tall Scot said, "Now what have I done?"

Joan said, "I don't know if you've done anything amiss, my boy, but I'll tell you this — you're so daft about her, it doesn't make sense. We hardly know her."

He brushed her hand off his arm impatiently and would have responded when a group from the anteroom burst into the party.

"Hail, hail, the gang's all here — at least the best part of it is!" The young man who had greeted newcomers at the front door was thrusting a new arrival into the room. "Have a good look, folks! Here he is! The dapper, the devilish, the devastating Professor Richard Fayne!"

"Assistant Professor," Richard said.

"I don't believe it!" Kristin said to Alexa.

"Neither do I." Alexa eyed Richard Fayne appraisingly. "I forgot how good-looking he is. No wonder you've got such a fix on him!"

"That's ridiculous! I don't have —" She broke

off and reddened as Richard Fayne spotted her against the wall.

"Kristin! Fancy you being here!" He sounded genuinely pleased, shook hands with her warmly, and turned to Alexa. "Alexa, it's a nice surprise."

How handsome he is, Kristin thought. She, too, had forgotten what an attractive man he was. His dark hair, thick and crisp, his warm brown eyes, and that secret smile that seemed to dare her to shock him, to join him. She felt a strange flurry of emotion and didn't like it, intruding on her this way, embarrassing her in front of Alexa, who smiled knowingly at her while greeting him.

"I'm thrilled to meet you again, Mr. Fayne," Alexa said sarcastically. She would have added more, but Kristin threw her a look that silenced her.

"Please, 'Richard' is fine," he said.

In the next instant, someone turned on the hi-fi and someone came up to Alexa and asked her to dance. Kristin and Richard Fayne were alone.

"I'm not very good at this." He waved his hand vaguely toward the music and the dancers. "Shall we give it a try?"

She went into his outstretched arms nervously. *If he's not very good, we'll make fools of ourselves.* It wasn't that she didn't know how to dance. There just seemed to be enough of a difference in how these Europeans danced that could possibly make it awkward. But her anxiety quickly vanished. It was too exciting being so close to this tall, dark stranger. She felt the rough texture of his tweed jacket, her cheek was almost touching his. His hand was smooth and hard and held hers firmly as he led her across the floor. They managed somehow to stay in step with the rhythmic beat of the music as they danced their way through the crowd.

"You're a very good dancer," Kristin said, accusingly.

"You're only saying that to be sweet," he said, adding with what Kristin took to be sarcasm, "American girls can be very sweet." Then, noting her small grimace of displeasure, "What's the matter? Have I offended you? I didn't mean to."

Oh, didn't you? Kristin thought. She felt he was testing her, playing a little game of cat and mouse, trying to arouse her interest. Well, she was no mouse.

"In America — and I suspect in a lot of other places — 'sweet' is anything but a compliment." She looked at him levelly.

"How so?" His eyes crinkled with amusement.

She hated his lofty, superior air. "When a girl isn't very good-looking or is clumsy or dull, people dismiss her with, 'She's sweet.' " She let that sink in. "And when it's a man"— she stared close into his eyes —"they say, 'He's nice.' " It came out almost angrily, which she hadn't intended.

He flashed her a delighted grin. Then he said quietly, "Kristin, you're a puzzle to me. And I don't know whether it's because I'm Scottish and you're American"— his dark brown eyes held hers —"or just that I want you to be a puzzle."

His arm tightened about her and he said nothing more as they danced close. She felt the beat of his pulse in the hand holding hers, an identical but fainter surge where the curve of his throat met her forehead. She listened to the quiet double beat, responding to his nearness, aware of the strange joy of this moment. She glanced across the room toward Alexa.

"What is it?" Richard said to Kristin.

"I don't know. She wants me." She stopped dancing, took his hand, and led the way toward Alexa.

"Look!" Alexa said breathlessly. "The necklace! She must have dropped it when she left the party!" Dangling from Alexa's hand, the pretty stones sent off flashing opalescent beams.

"Where'd you get this?" Richard's face was dark, threatening. Towering over Alexa, he seized the necklace.

"I found it. Here, on the sofa. It belonged to the blonde girl," Alexa said uncertainly.

"Who? What girl?" He stared fiercely at her.

"I saw her, too," Kristin said quietly. "She was blonde, very pretty. She was wearing it when she danced for everyone." She looked at him questioningly. "What's wrong?"

"Nothing. You'll have to excuse me. I'm leaving." He thrust the necklace into his pocket. "Forget this. I'll take care of it."

Without another word — *Nothing*, Kristin thought bitterly — he was gone.

* * *

"Why did he run out like that?" Alexa demanded. "If you ask me, the man is nuts, off his rocker, freaked out, and ready for a straitjacket."

It was the next morning. They were sitting in a sunny little restaurant on Queen Street, having breakfast. There was a basket of fresh-baked bread and rolls and scones and biscuits — warm from the oven, the usual pots of fruit jam and dairy fresh yellow butter, and steaming tea. They had found the coffee in Great Britain disappointing so far and had settled for tea, which was delicious wherever they ordered it.

"Please," Kristin said urgently, "I don't want to hear another word about him! What I want to do is keep one thing in mind, and one thing only — or I'll never find my mother!"

"Don't worry. We'll find her, Kristin, I know it. I know it!" She gave her friend a penetrating glance. "But don't fool yourself, Kristin. You're half in love with Mr. Dr. Professor whatever-you-call-him Fayne. And if you ask me —"

"I'm not asking you." Kristin set her cup down hard on the little tabletop and squared her shoulders. "I don't want to hear another word about him. Do you hear? He's out of my life. And that's where I want him to stay!"

"Okay, okay. Don't get frantic." She stopped and looked at Kristin. "But the angrier you get, the more I think you've really got a case on him."

"Stop it!" Kristin's voice rose dangerously. "Cut it out, Alexa! All I care about is my mother. My mother is missing! Missing! I don't want to talk about another thing except how can I find her!"

Her self-control broke and she began to cry. People at nearby tables watched as Alexa reached across the table and squeezed Kristin's hand.

"Oh, Kristin! Please forgive me. Of course your mother is all that counts!"

Kristin wiped her eyes. "I apologize, Alexa. I'm a nervous wreck. And a mean one — taking advantage of you and your parents."

Alexa said, "That's crazy and you know it. What we're going to do now is go straight to the university and track down your mother, step by step — from the moment she walked away from there for the last time." Alexa clapped a hand to her mouth. "I didn't mean that, Kristin. I meant when she left school for the last time —" She broke off.

"It's all right, Alexa." Kristin stood up.

Together they left the restaurant and walked out into a brilliantly sunlit day. Around them were happy people, enjoying the warmth and the sunshine.

But in Kristin's heart there was a cold lump of sorrow, of fear. *My mother. Where is she? Where is she?*

She could think of nothing else.

The young woman walked into the room and looked down at the woman lying there. She nudged her with her foot.

"Get up," she said. "Sit up. You've got to start writing again."

"I can't. Too weak," Margaret Clark said. "I can't hold a pen in my hand."

"No excuses," Pamela said. "I got you the papers you said you needed. Now start writing."

"It won't work." Margaret's voice was barely a whisper. "I can't say that your relative, Eunice Brown, wrote the Brontë manuscripts. Even if I wanted to do it, they'd send experts in to examine the pages. They'll establish through the pen and ink and the quality of the paper that —"

"Quiet!" Pamela said. "I tell you I won't listen to that kind of talk. Maybe you're in with them, is that it?" Her eyes glinted dangerously.

Margaret Clark said hastily, "No, no! Of course I think your family should get the credit they deserve. I only want to point out that it isn't up to me . . ." Her voice trailed off and she felt dizzy again.

"You've dallied long enough," the young woman said. "I've brought you everything you said you needed; now time is racing ahead. You write out the paper. Start now, do you hear?"

"I need more light," Margaret said.

"I can't give you any more than the candles," Pamela said. "Can't let those outside see we're in here." She leered at her captive. "They'll take the manuscript away from us. Can't let them do that, can we?"

No use trying to reason with her, Margaret thought. She's beyond that. She's completely obsessed. Aloud, she said, "No, we can't. Hand me the pen, and I'll try again."

The woman Pamela smiled crookedly and said, "Now that's a good girl. You go on writing and

I'll see that you've a good nourishing meal tonight."

"I've got to have help for my leg," Margaret Clark said, indicating the leg, now grossly swollen.

"All in good time," Pamela said. "When you've finished the paper."

CHAPTER 6

The big gray building loomed up like a mountain of stone at the top of the narrow road.

"I don't know," Kristin said. "Maybe this isn't the building where my mother taught."

"What difference does it make? We'll find out inside," Alexa said reasonably.

In that instant the door swung open and a tall, dark-haired figure stood before them, blocking their way.

It was Richard Fayne.

"Why, Kristin! And Alexa!" He stopped in his tracks, then grinned broadly. "This *is* a surprise! A most pleasant one."

He looked down at Kristin and his eyes brightened.

Kristin thought soberly, *Oh, no, you're not going to turn me on and off with your charm. Not this time.*

"It's nice to see you, Richard," she said. "We were just going in to make some inquiries about my mother."

He raised his eyebrows. "Your mother?"

"Yes. Dr. Margaret Clark. English Lit. She did the summer semester here. That's why I came to London — to meet her when the term ended."

Richard Fayne's smile vanished. His eyes flashed with something: recognition? anger? fear? Kristin couldn't identify it, but it shook her.

"But I *know* your mother, Kristin. I know her very well!"

"You do?" It was Kristin's turn to be surprised.

Other students were trying to get through the doorway. Richard Fayne took Kristin by the elbow and said, "Come inside. We can talk better in my office."

He led the way across a huge, high-ceilinged corridor that seemed more like the grand entrance hall to a castle than to a university. They went up a flight of steps and stopped at a door on which were the words, TWENTIETH-CENTURY AMERICAN LITERATURE.

He smiled as the girls read the sign. "Your mother and I were colleagues, Kristin, with widely varying interests — and therefore able to help each other. She's a brilliant woman."

Inside the small room, they sat down while he plugged a small electric plate into the wall and put a teakettle on, bringing forth three cups, a honey pot, and a tin of biscuits.

"We'll have tea in just a few minutes. Now what's this about your mother?"

Kristin felt an uneasy twinge — a feeling, however indistinct, that he was being devious.

"I never had a chance to speak to you about it. I didn't know you were a professor in this university."

"But didn't you say your name is Mulroy?" he asked, puzzled.

"Yes. It's also my mother's married name. But she was already well known under her maiden name — Margaret Clark — before she met my father, and she's always been a feminist, even before they had a name for the women's movement. So —"

"So she didn't want to lose the benefit of all the work she'd already done and she kept her maiden name. Right?"

"Exactly." Kristin shifted in her chair. "We're here, Richard, to try to find out what's happened to my mother."

Again that instant flash of his eyes. Alarm. This time she was certain. He said, "What do you mean? She told me she was going down to London to meet her daughter. I never dreamt it was you. Has she had an accident?"

"No," Alexa said. "At least we don't know. All we do know is that" —she hesitated — "she never arrived at the Daley."

He was instantly concerned. "When were you due to meet her, Kristin?"

"Well, I met you on Friday night after I got there, remember? She was due that day, or at the latest, the next day, Saturday." Her voice caught. "I waited till Sunday, but she didn't come. And I haven't heard from her. Not a word."

"I know very little, but maybe I can fill you in a bit." He got up, took the whistling kettle from the stove, and brewed a pot of tea. Then he came back.

"Your mother told me last week — let me see, it was Monday or Tuesday — that she was leaving for London to meet her daughter" — he nodded at Kristin — "but that she was going to take a side jaunt for a bit of research."

Again he seemed to Kristin to be withholding something. It was so strange. At one moment she felt she could trust him completely; the next, he was secretive. Why? Was she imagining it?

As if he could read her thoughts, he said, "If I sound a little vague, it's because I truly don't know exactly which day she planned to leave." His face darkened again. "Another thing, she was going off with someone else on the expedition. She didn't tell me who it was, but then I learned it was one of her students. I'm not sure which one."

"Please tell me everything you know," Kristin said. "My mother would never let three days go by without getting in touch with me somehow, if she could." Again tears welled in her eyes.

"Oh, I say, you poor girl. Of course you're upset!" He rose from his chair and came around to her side of the desk with the teapot. "Here, let me pour you a fresh cup. And have a biscuit with it. You too, Alexa."

Kristin shook her head almost angrily. "I don't want any more tea, thank you. I've got to get started somewhere, somehow." She started to push her chair back, when Richard Fayne snapped his fingers and said, "I know! I remember something!"

She looked at him hopefully. "Yes?"

"Loch Morland! I remember that very clearly. She told me that was the starting point of her journey." He scratched his chin. "I must say your mum was rather secretive about the whole trip."

Kristin smiled and thought, *Well, I'm not going to tell you anything. She said it was secret.*

"Have you been to the dormitory where your mother stayed?"

"Not yet."

She saddened, remembering her mother's words: "It'll be fun to be in a small room with a little desk and a single bed and books and papers all around. Like my student days in college."

Tears started to her eyes, but she blinked hard, swallowed, and said, "Is there anything else my mother said to you, Richard? Even the least thing might be a help."

Again his eyes were guarded. "Not at this moment. I'm sorry, Kristin. But talk to Mrs. McNair. She's the housemother in charge of the dorms. She may know something."

Suddenly he put an arm around Alexa's waist, the other around Kristin's, and said, "Come on, you two. I'll take you there."

Outside he led them to a square red brick building and introduced them to the housemother.

"She up and left on Wednesday week, she did. She said she wouldn't be back. She left me a forwarding address to the Hotel Daley in London, and that was that." She looked at Kristin warmly. "A dear woman, your mother. No airs about her for all that she's a famous professor from America. She's all right, I trust?"

"Yes," Kristin lied, with a warning look at Richard. "You're sure she left no note or mail for me?"

"No, as I said, the only thing was the address of Daley's."

Out in the street, Richard Fayne said, "I wish I could've been more helpful. As it is, I'm afraid you've only hit a dead end."

Kristin hesitated. "Not quite. There are one or two things I'd like to look into." He seemed curious, but she simply said, "Thank you again. I appreciate it."

"I'm sure you're welcome," he said uncertainly, then looked somewhat disappointed as Kristin and Alexa walked down the hill toward Queen Street once more.

"Now what was that all about?" Alexa asked. "You were rude enough to him for a change."

Kristin said, "I hope so. I can't stand his on-again, off-again moods. No matter how sweet he was just now, I wasn't about to walk into another one of his temperamental fits. I don't trust him."

"I'll admit that he's strange," Alexa said. "But that man is something special, Kristin. He really likes you, I can tell." When Kristin didn't answer, she said, "He doesn't pay any attention to me. I honestly think —" She broke off as she saw that Kristin didn't want to discuss it. "But I'd like to know something. What things are we going to follow up? You know — what you told him."

Kristin said, "Oh, I made that up. I didn't want him feeling sorry for me. But there's not much I can think of at this point. Nothing. *Nada.*"

She felt desperately low as they turned onto the beautiful main street of the city. They walked in silence past lovely buildings — some hotels new and modern, some others ancient landmarks, and some shops, chic and bright with fashionable clothes and household objects and other items to entrance the throng of tourists in the street.

Kristin's heart was leaden. What a foolish notion she'd had in London to come up here. What big plans! She was going to find her mother. She would do better than the police in London. Big deal. She was at a dead end. She hated this feeling of despair.

Then she thought of how her mother spoke to her when she felt this way. How you mustn't let *being* down *keep* you down. Slowly she felt some confidence returning. She remembered the pep talks they'd given each other. She would *act*. But where would she start?

Inspiration came to her. She seized Alexa by the arm and said, "Come on!"

Alexa, astonished, said, "Where?"

"You'll see."

They hurried down the avenue until Kristin pointed to a large red brick terminal perhaps three streets away.

"The railway terminal. I want to find out which train goes to Loch Morland and how long it takes."

There was no train. They had to take a bus, and they couldn't leave until eight-thirty the next morning, but Kristin felt much better, because at last they had begun to take action.

Loch Morland was surely one of the most beautiful towns on earth. They arrived in the picturesque little village, with its narrow winding streets and charming little shops, promptly at ten.

"I thought about it all last night," Kristin said. "I looked up the names of possible places my mother would stay." She pulled a list out of her jacket pocket. Both girls were wearing trench coats. They had learned in their brief time in England and Scotland that rain — anything from a light shower to a heavy deluge — could strike at any time. They also carried umbrellas and, in their tote bags, light boots, in case a charming little shower suddenly turned into a cloudburst.

"Look. There's one of the three hotels or inns or guest houses my mother would choose." Kristin indicated a small, cozy, oak-timbered Tudor-style building five or six doors away, down the incline of a cobblestone street. "Come on."

The clerk at the desk of the Olde Boar's Head was a sweet little man of about sixty who was terribly sorry when he didn't have the information they wanted.

"Hmmm . . . Clark, you say? Margaret Clark?" He flipped the pages of a registry book that only too plainly had very few names listed for the previous week. "Let me see." He made a big business out of pretending to search through dozens and dozens of names. It was pitiful. Kristin decided to put him out of his misery.

"I guess she didn't stay here," she said. "Thank you for taking such trouble."

Out in the street, Kristin stopped and said, "I have a definite feeling the tourist season is practically over."

"I don't blame them. I mean the tourists." Alexa shivered in the bracing cold air and drew her trench coat more tightly about her. "There's a lot to be said for a tropical island." She stopped and sneezed. "I think I'm getting pneumonia." She sneezed again.

"We won't be too long," Kristin said. "I promise you. But I've *got* to check out every possibility." She consulted the list in her pocket. "The Pork Pie. That's the next stop."

They had no more luck at the Pork Pie than at the Olde Boar's Head. "Nae, we've had nae American ladies stop over," the owner of the inn told them. "It's just about due time for the end of the tourist business." He looked rather sad as he said it.

Outside, Kristin said, "Let's get a newspaper and look up rooming houses. Maybe my mother and that student stayed there."

"Good idea." Alexa was humoring Kristin. But then, she defended herself, why not? Kristin was a wreck. And who could blame her?

Alexa was thinking of all the dire things that might have happened to Kristin's mother, as Kristin stopped at a newsstand outside a stationery store.

"Oh, my God," Kristin said in a voice hushed with terror. "Look at that!"

A shudder traveled up Alexa's body. The black, bold headline of the *Daily Telegraph* read:

TWO WOMEN DROWNED IN LAKE
BODIES STILL UNIDENTIFIED

CHAPTER 7

"Let me see!" Kristin's voice was shrill, verging on hysteria.

She grabbed the top newspaper and read aloud: "The two women found drowned in the lake last Thursday have still not been identified. 'The older woman,' the coroner states, 'was in her late forties —' "

Kristin broke off. "Oh, no! It can't be!"

"It isn't," Alexa said fiercely. "I know it isn't. Let's find out now. Let's go to the police!"

Ten minutes later they were in the police station, which looked more like a little store with green glass windows; two red globes outside were the only indication that this was police headquarters. The police force was Captain Shadrock and his young nephew, an amiable-looking man in his early twenties.

"There's only one way to make sure, my dear girl," the police captain said. "And that is for you to make an identification." Then, seeing Kristin shrink, he added, "My nephew and I will go with you, of course. The bodies are in the wee house in back. I'm happy to say the mortician did a fine job. The town of Loch Morland will give them a decent burial, you may be sure of that."

He would have rambled on, but Alexa stepped forward. "You want us to take a look at the bodies, Captain? Is that it?" He started a verbose answer, but Alexa said to Kristin, "Kris, if you want, I'll do it. I mean, if you don't feel up to it."

Kristin, white as ashes, shook her head. "No, thanks, Alexa. I'll go. You don't have to come with me."

"You can't stop me!" Alexa said fiercely. She seized Kristin's arm and they followed the two men through a long dark hallway in the rear, then out into the raw, rainy day. Before them, surrounded by deep, wet loam, they saw a wooden shack, old and weatherbeaten, but sturdy enough. A huge padlock hung on the door; the captain fiddled with a ring of keys in an effort to open it.

"This house was built to be an icehouse seventy-five years ago. We use it whenever there's reason to store a body here for any length of time."

He seemed to go out of his way to give the gory details, Alexa thought. She wished he would shut up and let them inside. But he fumbled with the lock and the keys for several minutes, before the door gave way into a dark cubbyhole of a room. He said, "There you are. Now if you'll just step inside . . ."

The girls held back, largely because they couldn't see into the blackness of the room. Noticing, the man said, "Oh, yes, very dark in there. Can you fetch a flashlight, Joel?" This last to his nephew, who took out a flashlight and beamed it ahead. He took Kristin by an elbow into the cramped blackness of this death-cold house. Kristin walked into the room and stopped. She forced herself to look at a long wide table on which two forms lay covered by sheets. As the young policeman threw back the first sheet, Kristin dug her fingernails into his arm and peered into the gloom. But then she saw. The woman who lay there was not her mother. She was heavier, older, her features thicker, her hair darker — a perfect stranger. Kristin shook her head no. The young policeman walked her around the table to where the second figure lay. Again he threw the covering sheet back. Again Kristin forced herself to look. This woman was white-haired, even older than the first.

She could have fainted with relief. She shook her head at the young policeman, who covered the body and took Kristin away at once.

Outside again, after thanking the police chief and especially the young nephew, Alexa rushed Kristin through the little police station and out onto the main street.

Kristin was on the brink of hysteria. "Alexa, Alexa! Isn't it wonderful? I mean, I'm sorry for those poor women in there. And I hope the police find out who they are and what happened to them, but all I know now is — it's not my mother!"

Alexa, shaken, could say nothing.

"The first place I'm going when we get back," Kristin said firmly as they rode the bus back to

Edinburgh, "is the dormitory at the university. I've got to see where my mother stayed. I'm going to *make* Mrs. MacNair let us into that room."

"It's a very irregular thing you're asking of me," Mrs. MacNair said. "Practically breaking in, I am, with the young man not even in his room." She looked indignantly at Kristin. "Really, I don't know why I'm doing this for you."

Nevertheless, she unlocked the door. The small room held a narrow bed, a chest of drawers, a chair, and a small table.

As Kristin and Alexa went in, the housemother cautioned, "Now be quick about it." She looked nervously out into the corridor. "I shouldn't be doing this. It's as much as my job is worth."

"I appreciate it, I really do," Kristin said, busily surveying the cramped space.

There seemed to be nothing but a suitcase — obviously a man's — on the floor, with the lid flung open and various male garments jumbled inside. On the table were some masculine items — a razor, shaving cream, a comb and brush set. Nothing. There was also a pile of books, ten or twelve, on a corner of the table. Kristin was about to turn away when she stopped short at the sight of a slim, green volume.

She pounced on it, took it up, and yelled, "Charles Dickens! *Great Expectations!* With a dent in the binding. This is my mother's!" She showed the battered book to Alexa. "Look, that's where Chico grabbed it and chewed on it when he was a puppy. Mother walloped him — it's a rare old book she got from the dean last Christmas!"

She was elated by the find, but Mrs. MacNair was not impressed. "How do I know it's your mother's?" she asked.

Kristin showed her the inscription in purple ink on the flyleaf: *Margaret Clark, December 25, 1981, with deep admiration for a brilliant colleague, from Dean Halberstadt.*

"You've got to go now," the housemother said.

"Oh, please! Please give me just another minute to look around," Kristin implored.

Alexa suddenly went down on her hands and knees, picked up some scraps of paper from beneath the desk, and then sat back on her heels triumphantly. "Look what I've got! Found them right here under the wastebasket." Pleased with herself. "Whew! Your new roomer is hardly the neatest thing you ever saw," she told the housemother.

"Well," Mrs. MacNair said, mollified, "I will say Dr. Clark was a lovely tenant, a lovely person. But I can't let you rummage around like this. You must stop now."

Kristin was surveying the little pieces of paper eagerly. "Can't we take another look? This is part of something written by my mother. Don't you understand? Maybe it can help us find her."

Once more the good-natured woman let them look. She was so nervous they rushed through their search. But there was nothing more.

"Thank heaven," the good woman said, turning the key in the lock and pulling the door shut.

On the way downstairs, Kristin took a pound note out of her purse and put it in the house-mother's hand. "We're very grateful," she said.

The housekeeper said tearfully, "My dear girl, I hope you find your mother. I am sure that you will. I will pray that you do. Please let me know."

By now they were exhausted. They indulged themselves and took a taxi back to the Pink Heather, where the maid suddenly ran out and frantically waved at them.

"A phone call from London! I saw you through the window! I've got them on the phone now," she told them breathlessly.

Alexa rushed into the house and to the phone. She said, "Yes, Dad, we're both all right. . . . Where? Oh, we went off to Loch Morland. . . . Nothing important. But we're not giving up. . . . What? You want Kristin?"

Kristin picked up the phone. "You've got to come back to London," Mr. Bower said. "Alexa's aunt is here, as you know. Now her uncle has returned and wants to see her. Besides, you can't possibly stay alone in Edinburgh. We're in touch with the police here. . . . Nothing definite yet, but they're working on it. So be good, Kristin. Pack your things and come back with Alexa."

Kristin tried to protest, but Mr. Bower was adamant. After a few minutes, Mr. Bower said, "Now it's all settled, Kristin. You'll take the five-thirty train with Alexa. We'll pick you both up at the station late tonight."

"Great," Alexa said as they walked upstairs to their room. "I'm so glad we're not splitting up."

Inside, they started packing. Alexa was almost finished, and Kristin was halfway through as she lifted some clothes from the bureau drawer. She was about to put them into her suitcase, when she stopped with her arm in midair and said loudly, "No! Absolutely not!"

"What's the matter with you, Kristin? No? No what?"

Kristin flung the blouse down on the bed. "I'm not going back to London. I'm not. Don't try to make me!"

"But you've got to," Alexa said. "You told my father —"

"I can't run away now," Kristin said determinedly. "I've got to go on."

"But you've got nothing to go on with," Alexa said.

"How do I know?" Kristin said. She stuck her hand in her jacket pocket and pulled out her mother's book and the few scraps of paper Alexa had found in the room. "Look, Alexa, I almost forgot about this. It must mean something. Let's see."

She put the pieces of paper down on the tabletop and, ignoring Alexa's protests, shuffled them around in an attempt to match them. What she got was an almost unintelligible part of a message: *. . . indisputable proof . . . ocated in . . . own . . . of Chester, wher . . . vidence exi . . . that . . .*

"Listen, Alexa, *you've* got to go back to London. *I* don't. I'm going on further." She stopped and stared at her friend. "And since you're so curious, I'll tell you. I'm going to Chester."

"Chester?"

"It's a town in the north of England. A historic old town. I've heard my mother speak of it." She smoothed the few pieces of paper again. "This says there is proof located in the town of Chester."

"It doesn't have to mean that," Alexa protested.

"To me it does. Anyway, I don't care. It's a start. Maybe she went there. I'll try anything."

"You've never acted like this before," Alexa said. "I don't understand you anymore."

Kristin turned to face her friend. "Sorry, Alexa. But it's what my mother would do. She wouldn't quit. And I won't either."

In the end, Alexa gave in. Kristin was not returning to London, not just yet.

Nothing could budge her.

In the big old railway station in Edinburgh, Kristin loaded Alexa up with magazines and snacks for her trip. When she tried to pay the man at the newsstand, Alexa stopped her. "You're not paying. You'll need money where you're going."

Kristin said, "Okay, Alexa. You may be right."

"Let me lend you some money," Alexa said. "Please. You'll run short."

"No, Alexa. But thanks a million. Look, here comes your train," Kristin said. "Give my love to your parents." Suddenly she felt very forlorn. "I'm going to miss you like crazy."

"And me, you." Alexa was near tears.

They kissed good-bye, and Kristin started to walk slowly away, feeling depressed, wondering if she'd been stupid to part from Alexa, when she heard a deep voice calling.

"Kristin! Kristin Mulroy!"

She turned around to see Richard Fayne. It was a shock. Still, she had to admit to herself it was strangely pleasant to see him there. With her heart beating faster than was comfortable, she managed to smile at him as he strode toward her. He was big and confident, and so attractive in his customary rough tweeds and turtleneck sweater that people turned to watch him admiringly.

"What are you doing here?" he asked. "We're always meeting unexpectedly."

Kristin had a faint uneasy feeling. "I might ask the same thing," she said. Then, realizing it sounded hostile, she added, "I just saw Alexa off."

"Oh, really?" he said. "I rather thought you two were going to travel together."

Again Kristin got that strange feeling. Was he probing? But why would he do that? His next remark disarmed her completely.

"Going back to the Pink Heather? Let me walk you back, Kristin. I'd like to hear what you've learned about your mother." He looked at her with concern. "Or haven't you learned anything more?"

A terrible twinge of sadness assailed her. "Nothing," she said. "The trip to Loch Morland was a waste."

"Oh, that's too bad," he said. "Tell me, what will you do next?"

She felt that it was unwise to tell him her plan, but in the end she couldn't hold back. His piercing brown eyes demanded the truth; maybe she was a fool, but she told him about finding the note and about her plan of going to Chester.

This last seemed to surprise him. "Chester? Well, isn't that a coincidence! I'm driving there tomorrow, on business."

"You are?" Kristin said increduously.

"It's a fact," he assured her. "Chester is a rare, historic old town. One of the oldest in England. The Romans held it in the year 72 A.D. Then the Anglo-Saxons captured it, built high walls around the city, and held them off." He smiled that warm, thrilling smile. "But you'll see for yourself tomorrow. I'd like to drive you there, Kristin."

"Well . . . thank you," she said. *How did I get into this?* she wondered, as they came to the front gate of the Pink Heather.

"I can't understand why you haven't gotten any solid information about your mother by this time. I wish I knew who it was exactly that she went off with. She mentioned that it was a student at the university." He looked grimly at her. "I could kick myself for not having asked her who it was. That would be a help."

Kristin hesitated. "I'm not sure she'd have told you, Richard. She was keeping everything very secret, because she thought she was on the trail of something big."

"Typical professor's obsession." Richard shook his head. "The best of them — and believe me, Kristin, your mother is among the very best — sooner or later begin to believe they're about to make the Big Discovery. Too bad your mother let it happen."

"I don't know," Kristin said defensively. "It might be something important."

Richard looked at her. Then he said, "Well, we'll know soon enough, I'm sure." By this time they had reached the Pink Heather.

He walked her inside and into a small dark entrance hall. "It's a three-hour trip to Chester. I'll pick you up here at nine-thirty tomorrow morning. Or is that too early for you?"

"No, it's fine," Kristin assured him.

"Then I'll be getting back to my place," he said, but he waited there in the hallway.

The thought flashed through her mind, *I don't even know where you live, Richard. I don't know anything about you really.*

They stood wordlessly in the small dark anteroom, and Kristin felt an electric tension between them. This man had a terrific attraction for her; she felt vulnerable in an unaccustomed way. They were still for a long moment, then the door opened and someone came in.

Richard glanced at his watch. "How the time does pass! I'll see you in the morning, Kristin." In a moment he was gone.

Kristin had a light dinner at the inn and went back up to her room. She laid out her outfit for the morning. She packed her bag, got undressed, and was about to get into bed, when she opened her purse and took out the framed double picture of her mother and herself. She looked at her mother's picture for a long time, then kissed it tenderly, and put it back in her bag. She felt better, as if there were some connection to her mother, keeping her picture with her during these awful days.

She got into bed but could not sleep. Two thoughts crossed like daggers in her mind. Above all, there was the nagging terror of what might have happened to her mother. The other was Richard Fayne — his charm, his apparent kindness, and then, the mistrust she felt toward him.

What was he? An ordinary man or . . . a villain?

Then the terrible possibility crossed her mind. Could it be that he knew something about her mother's disappearance? Did he really have to go to Chester tomorrow or was he simply using that as an excuse to follow her?

CHAPTER 8

The little camper was snug and warm as they took off down the tree-lined street, turned right and left and right again, and entered the highway leading out of Edinburgh toward the south.

He was a superb driver, maneuvering the camper deftly along the highway, alert to the vagaries of the other drivers.

"Comfortable?" he said.

"Very. Please don't worry about me," she said. "And forgive me if I seem absentminded. But I do have so much on my mind. It's like living in a nightmare. I never knew exactly what they meant by that. Now I know." She shuddered. "It's awful."

"It's understandable, of course. But I hope — I'm sure — you'll clear up the mystery soon. I have a strong feeling that you'll make good headway in Chester, Kristin. No point hanging around Edinburgh with your mother gone," he said.

"*If* she's gone. She may still be there, but where?" Kristin sighed heavily. She punched a fist against her knee. "I've got to find her! I've got to!"

"You will," he said, reassuringly. He hesitated. "I'll do anything I can to help you, Kristin. I want you to know that you can count on me."

He said this so oddly that she turned to look at him. His profile was strong as he intently looked at the road. Then he turned toward her for a moment.

"Trust me," he said simply. "I want to help you."

He looked back at the road, and she stared at that rock-hard profile again. He seemed so honest, so reliable. But his actions were anything but reliable. From the moment she'd met him at the Hotel Daley — making a date for tea with her, then dashing off so inexplicably — he'd been a mystery. And again at the party in the Pink Heather, one moment dancing with her, friendly, warm — then gone like a flash, without a word of explanation.

And now, this chance meeting near the railway station.

He's holding something back, she thought. *I know it.*

Which led her back to her mother. Where could she be? It was incredible. Margaret Clark had no money to speak of; they both just struggled along on a professor's salary. If anyone wanted to spirit her mother away, money was not the motive.

An accident? But accidents got reported sooner or later. Thank heaven she and Alexa had gone up to Loch Morland, and she'd seen for herself that it was not her mother who had met that dreadful, watery fate.

Where are you?

She heard herself asking the question over and over in her head, knowing that her mother would answer her if she could. If not an accident, maybe she was ill, so ill that she could not make contact with anyone. And if not, if she'd been deliberately sidetracked by someone, then who? And why?

She looked again at Richard's cold, clear profile and thought, *I don't trust you, mister, not one bit. But I'll pretend that I do, and maybe keep some connection to my mother, wherever she is.*

As if reading her thoughts, he turned to her, and said, "You must know that I'm as upset as you are about your mother. I am, Kristin. But I also know that these things clear up much more quickly than one imagines." He added, casually, "What do you think could have happened to her? Got any theories?"

"No, Richard. Not a single one that matters," she said in a small, defeated voice.

"Want to try them out on me?" he asked.

What's he up to now? Should I tell him about mother's Brontë papers? About what her note said? Something told her to keep her peace.

"I'd rather not think about it now, if you don't mind," she said. "Maybe later, when we've reached Chester."

He shrugged. "All right with me," he said. "Jolly good. Your wish is my command."

It made for an uncomfortable ride now. Each was self-conscious, making an effort, however, to say something every now and then to break the dead silence. Kristin had never felt more ill at ease. From the few glances she stole at Richard, she could see that he too was finding the ride difficult.

Outside of Chester, both of them gave up all efforts at conversation. Kristin wished she had never agreed to come. She could have taken a train or a bus, whatever. It would have been better to be alone in her misery than sitting beside this stern-faced stranger, who, for all she knew, might actually have information about her mother and be suppressing it, keeping her in the dark. The thought was too awful.

He knows something, she thought. *And he's keeping it from me. Why? And what is it? He's up to no good.*

Kristin was so enchanted by her first sight of Chester that she burst out of her mood exuberantly. "It's gorgeous!" she cried.

They came upon the town of Chester over a hill from which they could see the beautiful river Dee, the stone-walled streets and the marvelous walk across the tops of the stone walls, the castlelike buildings, the beautiful stone towers, and the guardhouses posted every few blocks. The greenery was lush and thrusting upward in that special British Isles way. "We're old! Thousands of years old!" the trees and grass and bushes seemed to be saying. "Look at us! You can't make another spectacle like this anywhere." It was true.

"What a beautiful town!" Kristin said excitedly as they drove through the main street. Many of the buildings had shops on the street floor of an arcade with a roof overhead. There were restaurants, little shops, a big department store, and churches. Then Richard turned the camper into a semicircular driveway two blocks away from town and stopped in front of a small, low-hung, timbered inn. KING'S HEAD INN, said the gilt-and-brown wood sign out front.

"Why are we stopping here?" she asked. "Is this where you're going to stay?"

"It's where we're both going to stay," Richard said, still in that cool, detached manner he had assumed hours ago when they had stopped talking. "That is, unless you have something else in mind."

She didn't know what to say. She wanted to blurt out the truth: "I don't know what kind of place this is, how much does it cost, I haven't very much money, and what do you mean by 'we'?"

"It looks fine to me," she said. Then she got up enough courage to add, "I hope it isn't too terribly expensive."

He didn't let her finish. "It's in the same price range as the guest house you were staying in back in Edinburgh. How does that suit you?"

He had opened the door and was taking his bag and her suitcase out. Now he waited impatiently for her answer.

"It's fine," she said. "Thank you." She bit her lip to keep from saying more. What was wrong with this man? One minute friendly as anyone could hope for. Then lapsing into coldness, showing his annoyance clearly. *I hate him*, she thought as she followed him into the inn. She couldn't wait to be alone in her room and relax. She felt oddly queasy — it could have been from not having slept well and taking this long ride. It could have been nerves. In her entire life she had never felt so abandoned. What was she doing here with this strange man in this strange town somewhere in the north of England, while her mother was God knows where?

She brushed a hand across her forehead as she signed the register: *Kristin Mulroy, Wellsport, Indiana, U.S.A.* Before she could look at the rate card the registration clerk held, Richard Fayne reached over and said, "I'm a professor. Edinburgh University. I suppose there will be the usual discount rate for this student and me?" The clerk nodded and Richard signed the registry book.

"Room 21 and Room 23," the clerk said, handing the keys to them.

Kristin, thoroughly weary, trudged up the flight of heavily carpeted stairs, unaware by now of her surroundings. She could not wait to get into her room to lie down.

At the door of Room 21, the chamber boy threw open the door and said, "You've got the king's own bedroom, Miss."

When Kristin looked at him wonderingly, he

said, "This 'ere is where King Charles the First once spent a few days before he got his head chopped off." The boy took an index finger and slashed it across his throat swiftly.

Kristin shuddered. She handed the boy a twenty-pence piece and said, "Thank you." Richard stood nearby, watching her curiously.

"Are you all right?" Richard asked.

"I'm fine. Fine," Kristin said. "I'll see you later."

The door closed behind her and she leaned wearily against it, thinking, *I've never been so tired in my life. Got . . . to . . . lie . . . down.*

The small room was wood-paneled with crude, wide, rough-hewn logs, its ceiling so low the tip of her head almost touched it. A small gabled window with shutters half-screening the greenery beyond was so tiny it looked like it belonged in a fairy tale.

The bed was double size. A plump patchwork quilt was the only color in the room. Kristin took one look at the bed, the thick white pillows invitingly piled at the head. Never had anything looked so good to her in her life.

She kicked off her shoes, pulled back the quilt, and fell into the bed, resting her head, which felt dizzy and light, on the soft white pillows. In a moment she was in a deep, deep sleep.

She was dreaming that she was on a ship at sea. Somewhere, soft bells were clanging out the hours — *one! two! three!* She had begun to lose count when she awoke with a start. She looked around the strange, dark room and could not get her bearings. Where was this place? Not in Wellsport. Definitely not. Then where? Her mind whirled foolishly and stopped. *England. London. Chester!*

She sat up abruptly. She heard a clock sounding — *bong! bong!* So that was it. She had incorporated the clock into her dream. Then she heard the soft knock on the door. Her heart began to beat quickly; she felt the racing pulse in her tongue, her mouth, her head. She was overcome by a feeling of uncertainty. Again the rapping on the door sounded. She got up, swayed slightly, went to the door, and said, "Yes?" Her voice was like a child's, a weak treble sound.

"Open up! It's Richard! Are you all right?" the voice from the outside said.

She put her hand to her eyes, shook her head to clear it, and said, "Yes," as she turned the key in the lock to open the door.

He stood there, big and confident. His shadow against the hall light behind him was somehow ominous.

"I said, are you all right?" His voice was harsh.

She stood there, uneasily groping for the door frame to steady herself. Her tongue felt thick in her mouth.

"Well, are you?" he asked again. "I've come by several times and knocked, but you never answered." He bent down and looked directly in her eyes. "I say, Kristin, aren't you feeling well? You look awfully pale."

She walked by him through the doorway and

said faintly, "I'm fine. Thank you," and started down the corridor toward the washroom. Then all of a sudden her knees gave way beneath her and that was the last she knew as she dropped unconscious on the worn old boards.

She awoke slowly out of a stunned sleep, and for a few moments did not realize where she was. Then the horror overcame her as she remembered.

The throbbing in her leg kept pace with the beat of her heart, only more insistently. Her leg was a huge protuberance that seemed to be no part of her body. She looked down in the dark and saw that it was swathed with some wet solution, dipped in filthy rags by the feel and odor of them.

What am I to do? *She began to moan with the same rhythmic beat of the throbbing in the enormous leg. The sounds were animalistic; she could not believe they came from her.*

Where was Pamela? What time was it? She saw a streak of light in the sky but it told her nothing. It could be evening, it could be morning, in this rainswept, cloudy place. It could be the height of the day, and who was to know?

The door opened. Silhouetted against a thin light from behind, the figure in the doorway said, "Good evening, Dr. Clark. And how is the work going?"

Margaret Clark forced her voice to be calm.

"I can't stay here much longer like this, Pamela. Surely you must realize that I need medical care."

"But I do know it. And I am taking care. That's fuller's earth solution on those lovely towels I've brought you. It cures infections."

Again Margaret controlled her panic, her anger. If there were any way to get through to this demented creature, she had to find it. She must devise a rational plan that would work, something that might touch some thread of the madwoman's mind.

CHAPTER 9

"Kristin! Are you all right?"

The voice sounded in her ears and it was like going to a movie, staying there for the second time, and coming right around to the scene you came in on in the beginning.

"Kristin! Answer me!" the voice said again.

Another voice, a woman's, said, "She's coming round now, poor thing. She looks real done in."

Kristin opened her eyes. The chambermaid was pressing a cool compress against her forehead and smiling down at her. "There, dear, you'll be fine now. Up and cheery and good as new."

Kristin tried to thank the friendly woman, but couldn't. The terrible tiredness was over her again.

"I think we should have a doctor look at her," Richard said, looking down with concerned eyes.

"She's just overdoing," the chambermaid said. "I'll wager that's what it is. These young tourists, they tramp around wanting to see and do everything and they run themselves down. That's what it is."

Richard helped her up from the floor and back into her room.

"I really don't need a doctor," Kristin said. She glanced over at the chambermaid. "You're right, Daisy. I'm overtired."

Richard touched her forehead with his hand. "I think we should take your temperature. I've got a thermometer in my room."

"I've got one, too," Kristin said. "If you insist . . ."

"I do," he said. "Where is it?"

"In my suitcase . . ." She sat up in bed. "I'll get it . . ." She felt giddy.

"You stay there," he said firmly. "I'll find it."

"If you won't be needing me," the maid said, "I'll be going."

He opened Kristin's suitcase. She was glad she'd taken time to pack her things neatly the night before; still, it was embarrassing to have him rummaging through her personal belongings.

He brought the thermometer to her and she put it in her mouth. Two minutes went by, and she removed it. "One hundred," Kristin said ruefully. "Almost normal."

He took the thermometer and checked it. "Right, not much, but it means you need rest and —" He broke off as a knock came at the door. He opened it to a smiling Daisy who was carrying a tray with a teapot and cups and a plate of thin English biscuits.

"A spot of tea might do you good," she said to Kristin. "That, and a good night's rest." She hesitated. "I brought some aspirin."

"Thank you," Kristin said. "I really appreciate it."

The maid left and Kristin sipped the tea. She had never felt so foolishly helpless in her life, not even when she'd been a small child. There was something about Richard that made her feel like a vulnerable child. She liked — and hated — the feeling at the same time.

Kristin finished the cup of tea and said, "I feel a lot better. I'm going to get up."

Richard said, "There, you look a lot better now."

He pushed his chair back and stood up at the very same moment that she got to her feet. They were close together in an awkward position. He looked fixedly at her; they stood that way for a long moment. Suddenly he reached out and drew her close.

In the next moment his lips were on hers. In this strangest of places, on this strangest of days, that kiss came to Kristin like a flash from another space, another time, in her life. She felt as if she could step back and see herself, the two of them, in close embrace.

But in the next moment she was fully aware. She was Kristin Mulroy and this man *was* a stranger. She pushed him away and said, "Don't," and he instantly stepped back. His face was flushed as he picked up the tray and said, "I'll take this downstairs."

He turned the door handle and said, not looking at her, "I'm sorry for acting the fool," and left.

Kristin, alone again, sat down. The happenings

of this past hour seemed part of a crazy dream. Only the presence of Richard Fayne had been very real. And his kiss still lingered on her lips.

This was no way for her mind to be working, no way for her to be feeling. She got up and looked out into the dark night and thought, *I've got to find her. Somewhere out there my mother is waiting. If she's alive.* Then came the further, awful thought. *And if she's not . . . ?*

When Kristin got up early the next morning, she dressed hastily, and took a quick bath in the old, scroungy bathroom at the end of the corridor. Then she hurried downstairs to the lobby.

As she walked into the dining room, Richard was finishing breakfast. He wiped his lips with a napkin and stood up as she came across the room where a waiter indicated a table near a window.

Richard nodded his head. "How are you today?" His voice was thoroughly contained, his manner coolly polite.

"I'm fine, thank you." She felt as if she were speaking to a stranger.

"I'll be busy all day. Some special research for next semester." He looked briefly at her. "Have you any plans?"

If he could be cold and unfriendly, so could she. "Oh, yes," she said with a faint smile. "There are a few places that I plan to visit."

He looked at her quizzically. "Then I suppose I'll be seeing you back here at dinnertime?"

"I suppose so," she said, adding, "But if not, thanks again for the ride down."

"Well, good luck today, Kristin." He cleared his throat. "Try to make it back here by six o'clock, if you can, won't you?" He was still polite, but she got the feeling he really didn't care. Well, she needed a full day in Chester. She might as well meet him once more if it came to that. In any case, she wasn't going to ride back to London with him. The trip down had been too uncomfortable, and now matters between them were hopeless.

Her first stop would be the English-Speaking Union in town — her mother had often spoken of the good work done by this organization, with branches in so many cities throughout the world. Maybe the Union would know where her mother was, what project she had gone off on. Maybe her mother had visited them, had told them her plans, where she was going next.

"You know my mother?" Kristin asked. "Really?"

Mrs. Linden, a gentle-voiced woman of middle age, nodded happily. "Why, she's an outstanding English literature scholar. She's one of the few American professors whose papers we treasure here at the English-Speaking Union."

It sounded promising. But in the end, the visit was futile. Mrs. Linden knew nothing about her mother's whereabouts.

"I had a letter from Professor Clark in July, from Edinburgh, I believe. She said she wanted to come down sometime — it would be about this time, I believe." Mrs. Linden shrugged.

"Something about checking on the history of a famous literary person. She didn't mention who it was by name."

"Could it have been one of the Brontës?" Kristin asked, thinking, *I know I'm probably betraying mother's secret, but I've got to know.*

"Well, of course. However, she never did come down for a visit." Seeing Kristin's expression, she asked, "Is something wrong?"

"No . . ." Kristin began, then stopped. She took a deep breath. "Oh yes. Yes, Mrs. Linden!" She trusted this woman and could hold back no more.

"I can't find my mother," she confessed. "She was supposed to meet me in London last Saturday and she never showed up."

"How dreadful for you," Mrs. Linden said. "You've had no word from her?"

"None at all. Nothing." Kristin wiped her eyes. "Please forgive me. I don't mean to burden you with my problems."

"You poor girl, tell me everything," Mrs. Linden said.

When Kristin finished, the older woman told her, "If I were you, I would go at once to the police. If there is any way of putting you in touch with your mother, they're the ones who can help you. The Chester police force is quite famous in England. They're especially good at finding missing persons."

For the first time since leaving London, Kristin felt a faint stirring of hope. Gratefully, she embraced Mrs. Linden.

"Let me know when you've found her," Mrs. Linden said as Kristin prepared to leave.

"Oh, I will," Kristin promised. "You've been wonderful."

A half hour later, Kristin approached the white stone building that housed the Chester police force. She opened a heavy wooden door and stepped inside, then walked up to the front desk and was about to speak to the officer in charge when she saw someone coming down the hall toward the front door.

It was the last person she would have expected to see there.

Richard Fayne.

For a moment he seemed taken aback. Then he said quietly, "Hello, Kristin. This *is* a surprise."

I'll bet, she thought. Aloud she said, "Isn't it? I thought you were going to do some research in town."

He flushed darkly, aware that the desk sergeant was listening to every word. "I thought I'd check on your mother while I was here."

"In *Chester*?" Kristin said unbelievingly.

He glanced at his watch. "I've got to run, Kristin. I look forward to seeing you at the inn this evening."

Before she could answer, he had slammed out the front door.

"Can I help you?" the desk clerk asked.

When she told him her business, he took her at once to the police chief.

Captain Foley, a huge, smiling man dressed

in a well-tailored police uniform, greeted her warmly.

After he heard Kristin's story, he said, "I'm not promising anything, young lady. But if the London police haven't come up with anything yet, and since it was a false trail you followed up to Loch Morland, that leaves Chester as a possibility — at least one that we can't ignore."

She said earnestly, "Captain Foley, I can't tell you how much I appreciate it."

"Just our job, young lady." He nodded toward the huge clock on the wall. "It's almost noon. Things are fairly slow right now. Four or five hours should tell us the story. Go back to your hotel and wait there. If we get anything before five o'clock, we'll call you there. Got that?"

"Yes, thank you. I'll be waiting. Do you think you'll have anything to tell me?" She couldn't help asking that.

"We'll do our best, Miss," he said. "That's all I can say."

Kristin walked into the street with a heavy heart. There was nothing more she could do right now. She would go back to the inn and wait.

She sat in the shabby, dreary lounge of the King's Head Inn and felt again she was in a strange dreamworld, a world where all memories of her life in Indiana, her school friends — everything — was obliterated.

She had one fixed idea in her head. *Where is my mother*? Tears sprang to her eyes as she sat toying with a lukewarm ginger ale. The English were certainly not very big on ice. They said after a while you got to like lukewarm beer and ale, if you stayed in England. Maybe. Soppy ginger ale was not her idea of a treat.

I've got to stop this. How often had her mother told her how fruitless it was to let your thoughts spill rampant through your mind? *Focus.* That was her mother's strong injunction when something important had to be done.

The clock in the corner struck five. Kristin started guiltily. She'd spent the entire afternoon sitting in the lounge! How had the time sped by like this? And no word from the police captain. What was she waiting for, anyway? She couldn't stay endlessly here in Chester while some small-town police officials poked around trying to find evidence of her mother's whereabouts. She stirred the warm drink in her glass and sipped a little. It was flat. How could English people drink slop like this?

There I go again.

Focus. *Focus*!

"Oh, there you are!"

She looked up and saw Richard Fayne.

"Hello, Richard."

It was difficult to keep her hostility from showing. There he stood, tall, ruddy, bright, friendly, exactly as if everything were perfectly normal.

He picked up on her mood at once. "You look awfully down, Kristin. Not bad news, I hope."

Was he mocking her? She was so angry she could have smashed his face.

He picked up on that, too. "I say, you seem annoyed. Is it something I've done?"

She could contain herself no longer. All the bitterness, the anguish, the weight of sorrow of these past days rose to her lips, and she did not try, could not have managed, to hold back.

"Annoyed? What are you talking about? Don't you have any sense of what people *feel?*" She had to stop, to keep her voice even. She saw the whites of his eyes widen in astonishment, setting off the dark turbulence of the pupils. She swallowed, forced herself to go on. She didn't care what he felt.

"You ask me if I'm annoyed? You must be crazy. My mother is missing. I'm alone in a strange country, a strange continent, and my mother is missing!"

He touched her hand. "I understand, Kristin. It's a dreadful situation. I would like to help you —" He broke off as she hastily pushed his hand off her arm.

"Oh, yes. I know. What you don't realize, Richard Fayne, is that you're the last person in the world I would go to for help!"

"I hope you don't mean that," he said quietly.

"I do! What reason do I have to trust you? You do such strange things. You say one thing and do another." She laughed bitterly. "No, thank you. I'll get by without your help."

He stood there for a moment, looking at her thoughtfully. Then he seemed to reach a decision.

"Kristin, I know that much of what you're saying is true. But much of it is beyond my ability to explain." He seized her shoulders firmly and drew her up from the chair. "Kristin, please trust me. Please."

"Why should I?" She wished he would not hold her like this. She couldn't think with those eyes meeting hers, Richard's whole face questing, anxious, so close to her own. No, she would not let herself be talked into any more of Mr. Richard Fayne's little games. She would not.

He put a finger to her lips. "Kristin, hush now." His voice had lapsed into the Scottish accent again. She could feel his finger on her lips, trembling. "Please, Kristin. Do me this one favor. I want to speak to you alone. But not here. I have my reasons."

"Reasons?" What was he talking about?

"Please have dinner with me tonight." He glanced at his wristwatch. "I know you're expecting word from the police." She wondered how he knew that, but said nothing. She would give no more information to this man. On the contrary, she would try to learn as much from him as possible.

"If you will come to dinner with me, I think it would be good for you, Kristin. You can't stay alone, brooding like this. I'll let the police know where we'll be and they can call you there, if that's what's worrying you."

"Of course it is," Kristin said. Could she believe him? What would it hurt to have dinner with him and hear what he had to say?

"I'll go with you," she said. "Is it far from here?"

"No, it's just down the street a short way." He smiled and squeezed her shoulder. "Thank you, Kristin. You won't regret it. I promise you that."

So it was arranged. She would meet him in the lobby in twenty minutes.

She left him and ran up the stairs to her room. There she tried to get her emotions under control. There was no doubt that Richard Fayne exercised a fascination for her. What was she thinking of? Nothing had changed. Richard Fayne was as slippery, as tantalizing as a wraith that came in the night and disappeared at will.

As she put on a bright blue silk dress, she thought, *There's no harm in looking my best. I won't let that man know I care for him. Alexa would do this.* She'd dress up to kill and flirt like a maniac, promising all sorts of romantic goodies that Kristin knew for a fact Alexa never fulfilled. Alexa was a girl who kissed and coquetted — and that was it. She could never commit herself to anyone, because she was so busy flitting from man to man like a passionate bumblebee. Not for her to develop a relationship with any one male.

Why do I have to be this way — looking for the same kind of commitment from a man that I'm able to give? Kristin asked herself as she stared into the mirror and brushed her hair in a flyaway style that suited her mood.

You know, you're nuts, she said to her reflection in the mirror. *All you're going to do is have dinner with Richard Fayne.*

As she walked down the steps, she thought, *If he even tries to hold my hand, I'll stop him right there.* Then she saw him standing there, waiting, dressed in a blue blazer with pale gray trousers, wearing a shirt and tie. She was glad she had decided to dress up. And she knew what she intended to get out of this evening.

"Good evening, Richard," she said, and held out her hand in greeting.

A look of pleased surprise sprang to his eyes and he took her arm. "You look lovely," he said.

Outside, he said, "I hope you like Chinese food."

"I love it," she assured him.

They walked down the street, passing small shops closed for the night, until they got to the main street, where they walked under the overhang along the Rialto until they came to a small, unpretentious-looking Chinese restaurant. Kristin saw him look back over his shoulder uncertainly as they entered the restaurant. But then he turned around and said, "You know, I gave the police this number in case they wanted to talk to you." Kristin had a definite feeling that he was trying to divert her attention.

Uncertainly, she sat down with him at a small candlelit table beside the front window. An Oriental man, dressed in a loose brocaded jacket and wide black silk trousers, smiling, handed them two menus.

"I know this place well," Richard said. "If you like, I can order for both of us. Just tell me what kind of dish you prefer — chicken, beef, shrimp . . . ?"

"I like all of them," Kristin said. "That's my problem. It's so hard for me to diet."

"You don't have to," he told her with an approving grin. "But since you've given me leeway, let's have the Chicken Orientale, a side dish of Butterfly Shrimp, Vegetables Polynesian — and fried rice, of course."

The waiter hurried away. Suddenly Kristin felt ill at ease with Richard. But she was determined that the burden of this evening would be on him, not her. Soon her strategy seemed to be working. When Richard spoke again, his assurance seemed to have left him.

"Kristin, I know you want me to explain a few things to you." His dark brown eyes were troubled. "A few of my appearances and disappearances, for example."

"That would be a help," Kristin said. "What are you really doing in Chester? I hate to say it, but I have a feeling that it has something to do with me — and my mother . . ."

Suddenly she felt ridiculous. *What kind of paranoia is this?* she thought. *Richard Fayne is a Scotsman, a young professor in Edinburgh. And we're in the British Isles.* It isn't like America, a huge country where it was unlikely you would meet people in unexpected places. The whole of the British Isles would be lost in just the state of Texas, for example.

"You're not far off target," Richard said as the

waiter, smiling, brought up a rolling cart with a myriad of covered dishes. He set them on the table and then left.

Kristin wished the food hadn't come just then. Richard had seemed about to open up. Now he was making light talk again as he served them.

"I think you'll like this food. They've got such a fantastic chef. I've been coming here ever since my student days. Tell me what you think." Richard finished spooning out the food on Kristin's plate and he waited, with obvious curiosity.

Kristin took a fork, speared a chunk of chicken, savored it a moment, and declared, "It's perfect. You didn't exaggerate one bit."

"See? I *can* be trusted," he said, pleased.

I wish I could believe you, she thought.

And then it happened.

She saw Richard glance out the window beside their table. It had begun to rain and people were hurrying along even though the overhang protected them from the downpour. But that was when Kristin saw her in the crowd, seconds before she disappeared completely — a young woman with blonde hair, wearing a belted trench coat, hurrying past.

Instantly, Richard leaped up. He snatched a handful of bills from his pocket and thrust them at Kristin.

"Here! This will pay for dinner," he said. "Sorry, I've got to go. See you back at the hotel — good-bye."

"Wait a minute! You *can't* do this again," Kristin said.

But he could, and did. He was out of the door and running down the street in the direction the young blonde woman had gone. Kristin had not seen the woman's face, but with a sinking heart she realized who it was, who it had to be.

The same girl who had danced so wildly only — what was it? Two? three? nights ago at the party in the Pink Heather in Edinburgh.

Who was she? More important — what was Richard's connection to her?

Back in her room, Kristin brushed angry tears away, walked to the closet, and pulled her suitcase down. Just as angrily, she rammed her clothes into the bag, when suddenly she noticed it.

A jagged slash in the lining of the suitcase. She pulled the clothes back and took a closer look. There was no doubt about it. This was no accidental rip.

It was a deliberate cut made by a sharp instrument.

CHAPTER 10

The blood surged to her head and then ebbed back into her body. Shaking, she clutched a chair and sat down.

Someone's been here. Who? When? How had whoever it was gotten in? While she was out having dinner with Richard? Earlier? Yesterday, when they first arrived?

She shook her head, terribly upset.

I've got to talk to someone.

On an impulse, she opened the door and hurried downstairs to the lobby. A middle-aged woman sat behind an old-fashioned telephone switchboard.

"Yes, mum? Can I help you?"

"Yes, if you please." The woman had a friendly face, so Kristin took a breath and said, "You see, I just got here last night. I've got a couple of questions . . ."

"Go right ahead," the operator said.

"Can you tell me if you've had many people check in since then?"

"I wouldn't know exactly, but there have been

a few new ones," the operator said chattily. "There's a man who came in late that night, I believe."

"Have you seen him? What did he look like? Was he dark-haired?" Kristin said eagerly.

"No, he was sort of tall and thin — a young fellow."

The telephone operator looked at Kristin curiously. "Why, dear, were you expecting someone?"

"No! I wasn't expecting anyone," Kristin said. "Can you remember anybody else who's new here?"

Even as she asked the question, Kristin realized how foolish it was. Anyone wanting to get into the hotel could do so without checking in. All a stranger had to do was go to the lounge downstairs, have a drink, and then, using the washroom as an excuse, have free entry with a master key to any room in the inn. It was the same in the United States. That's why there was so much crime in hotels. There was no possible way to check every floor and every room people went to. Not in any hotel. Surely not in a busy little inn like the King's Head.

". . . so you see," the operator was saying, "I don't think I can help you there."

Kristin waited, wondering what to do next, when the operator spoke again.

"But you do seem a bit troubled, dear. Are you sure there's nothing I can do?"

The woman's caring voice helped Kristin to decide. "Yes, thank you. You can put through a call to London for me. To the Quadro Hotel. I want to speak to Ms. Alexa Bower."

Pleased, the woman nodded and began to manipulate plugs and lights and cords. She finally turned to say, "I've got your party on the line now. Please use that phone over there."

Kristin picked up a small wall phone and heard Alexa. "Hello, hello? Who is it? Who's calling?"

"Alexa! It's me, Kristin! I've got to talk to you!" It was difficult trying to keep her voice low enough so the operator would not overhear.

Alexa was excited, asking so many questions Kristin had to stop her.

"Alexa! You remember what happened to me at the Hotel Daley the first night? Well, same thing . . . No, not the whole room — just my suitcase."

She told Alexa everything, not only about the slashed bag, but meeting Richard at the police station, his odd behavior, his desertion tonight after the blonde girl walked by.

"Really? The same girl! I can't believe it!" Alexa was appalled. "Kristin! You've got to come back to London right now. My mother and father insist. They think — and I do, too — that it's terrible, you wandering around by yourself all over England, and now — oh, what they'll say when I tell them about your bag?"

That gave Kristin an idea. "Alexa. That airline steward — have you seen him again?"

"No, I haven't," Alexa said. "But you'll never guess who I *did* see in the train station at Bingley on the way back to London!"

"Who?" Kristin held her breath, somehow knowing the answer.

"That Egyptian guy — you know, the gorgeous one."

"*Farouk*?"

"You've got it!"

"Where did you say this was?"

"I'm trying to tell you. In the station in Bingley. That's the first stop we made on the way back to London," Alexa said. "Kristin! What's wrong?"

"Plenty. Was he traveling to London on your train?"

"No, silly. He was on a train going the opposite direction — coming up from London. Our trains met, that's all!"

"That's it!" Kristin said. "That explains it."

"You mean, he's the one that slashed your bag?"

"Careful, Alexa." Kristin lowered her voice. "Please don't say any more."

"Why not?" Alexa persisted.

"Because he may be here someplace." Kristin's voice was a bare whisper. "I'm going to hang up now."

"You mean you think he could be listening in?" Alexa said incredulously.

"No more, Alexa. I'm going to hang up."

Before Kristin could say her final good-bye, another voice sounded at the other end of the phone. "Kristin Mulroy! This is Stella Bower. Now listen, Kristin, Mr. Bower and I are very disturbed. You cannot continue to put yourself in such danger! We want you to come back to London at once."

Kristin's heart sank. This *was* the voice of reason. She had accomplished nothing, and this last incident — the slashing of her bag — seemed to be still one more warning. She should leave Chester.

"Kristin? Kristin, are you there?" Mrs. Bower's high musical voice was anxious. "Now listen to me, dear —" and she launched into a long recital of reasons why Kristin should come back to them in London.

Conflicting thoughts raced through Kristin's head as Alexa's mother was speaking. Then, at last, she said wearily, "I'll come back, Mrs. Bower."

"Oh, that's wonderful! Now you're being sensible. When can we expect you?

"I'll make the late afternoon train. It gets into London around eleven o'clock." Then she added, "I appreciate your advice. I know I've made you worry. But my mother —"

"Don't say any more, dear. The police are working on the case and Inspector Chilton tells us that he expects some news soon." Mrs. Bower blew a kiss into the phone. "We love you, dear. Now be careful — and please don't worry anymore. We'll discuss everything when you get here."

Kristin hung up the phone to see the telephone operator looking quizzically at her.

"Thanks for everything," she said, before the

operator could start a conversation again. "I really appreciate it."

She walked away and up the stairs dispiritedly. In her room, she looked around, defeated. She began to repack her bag, slowly this time, thinking.

Alexa, Mrs. Bower — they're right. This is idiotic. Mother is wrong. I'm wrong.

If she ever doubted that before, she knew it now. Look at the Bowers. Mrs. Bower, protected and loved by her husband. Alexa. Both women safe in a lovely hotel in London. Mr. Bower making plans, looking after them.

And look at me and my mother. The two of us adrift in a nightmare situation like this. How often my mother told me: Act. Focus. Dare to do! *Now look at her, for all her achievements—she's God knows where. Or with whom. Or maybe even not alive.*

She gulped and forced back the tears and kept determinedly packing her suitcase, then closed it with a loud snap.

She went to the closet, took out her raincoat, picked up her tote bag and her purse. She opened the purse, took out the silver double picture, and stared at her mother intently, then sighed heavily and put it back in her pocketbook.

She took a final look around the room.

What a mess it's been. My room broken into in London, then off on a wild chase to Edinburgh. That crazy girl at the party. Richard — blowing hot, cold, vanishing at the drop of a hat. Now someone in my room here.

She could have cried with rage, sorrow, frustration.

She picked up the heavy bag and left the room. She started down the stairs with one thought in mind. She was going back to London — to safety. Her mother's philosophy about women's freedom had led them both to this. It had to stop someplace. Well, it was stopping now. She was going to London.

When she paid her bill at the desk, the clerk said, "Miss Mulroy! I have a message for you."

He handed her an envelope with the inn's name on it. "Professor Fayne left this for you." He watched curiously as she took the envelope, but she nodded her thanks and walked away to the lounge. There, she ripped the envelope open to find two five-pound notes and a brief message:

Dear Kristin:

Sorry to rush off like this. The enclosed, I hope, will help see you through to your return trip to London. I will try to be in touch with you at either the Daley or your friend's hotel — the Quadro? In any case, go back, Kristin, go back to your friends in London. There's only danger for you if you continue to search for your mother. I'll check with the police here as you wait for word from the police in London.

Regards,
Richard Fayne

Kristin read and reread the note before she gave vent to her feelings. The man was incredible. "Go back." "There's only danger for you if you continue to search for your mother." *He* would check the police. What a laugh! He couldn't be relied on to stay in one place, let alone follow through on a hunt for her mother. What a man! Kiss her, win her over, tell her he was her friend. Then dash off again, leaving "Regards." Signing himself "Richard Fayne." It was ludicrous.

In the lobby, she looked at the clock. More than enough time to get to the train station. An hour and a half. Well, she'd rather spend it here in the inn than in a cold, ugly station.

She settled down in a big, upholstered, red mohair couch. Beside her, a foot away, a heavy oak bookcase leaned against the ancient wall crammed with books. Her eyes idly roamed the shelves. *David Copperfield, Pride and Prejudice, Rasselas, The Complete Works of Shakespeare.* And a slim little volume, deep red Moroccan leather with gold letters—*Jane Eyre.* Beneath that, the name of the author, Charlotte Brontë. Something stirred within Kristin. She reached over and withdrew the book.

Brontë. The very name was enough to set her pulse racing. Why was her mother so interested in that accursed family? What were they all about, anyway, those Brontës?

She opened the book at random and her eyes fell on a paragraph:

> Women are supposed to be very calm generally: but women feel just as men feel; they need exercise for their faculties, and a field for their efforts as much as their brothers do; they suffer from too rigid a constraint, too absolute a stagnation, precisely as men would suffer; and it is narrow-minded in their more privileged fellow-creatures to say that they ought to confine themselves to making puddings and knitting stockings, to playing on the piano and embroidering bags. It is thoughtless to condemn them, or laugh at them, if they seek to do more or learn more than custom has pronounced necessary for their sex.

That's my answer!

It was incredible to have found it at this time. Her mind exploded into a dozen thoughts. *Of course my mother's life is a thousand times more exciting and meaningful than Stella Bower's!* Of course she, Kristin, was more alive, more aware than Alexa. Alexa, for all that she loved her, moved in a dreamworld padded with the comfort that money could buy. Alexa and her private school. Alexa and her fabulous clothes, her constant trips to the beauty parlor, her family's emphasis on appearance, meeting the right people — whoever they might be — keeping Daddy happy as her mother did. Nothing wrong in that, if Daddy spent as much time and effort keeping Mother happy. And not just with tangible things — clothes, fine furniture, jewelry. How about freedom of mind? Mrs. Bower's favorite reply to her husband was, "Whatever you think, dear." What a price to pay for those so-called luxuries!

Her answer lay in this slim red book, written by a young woman in her twenties, one hundred and fifty years ago. Of course she, Kristin, had to follow her own path, her destiny as a woman.

She hurried to the lobby and spoke to the desk clerk.

"Can you tell me where I can buy a copy of this?" She held up the red-bound copy of *Jane Eyre*.

The clerk laughed. "In any bookstore in Great Britain. It's a classic, you know." He was about to continue when he said, "Wait up! I do believe. . ." He fumbled beneath the desk. "Oh, yes, here it is." He brought up a cheap paperbound copy of *Jane Eyre*. "Someone left it here well over six months ago. I daresay you are welcome to it, young lady."

"Are you sure?" He nodded and Kristin took the book, pleased.

"You know, tourists to England visit Stratford-on-Avon — Shakespeare's birthplace — and Haworth in Yorkshire, up on the moors — that's the home of the Brontës. Those are the two most famous literary places in England that people come from all over the world to see."

That decided Kristin. She could not, would not listen to the Bowers. She and her mother were different people from the Bowers. Maybe their road was dangerous, surely it was lonely, and above all, it was often heartrending. But to

Haworth she would go. *Now*. The Brontës were her mother's special major interest in her field of work. That was what had lured her off on her mystery trip. Kristin would go there now and look for some answers.

But first she would phone the Bowers in London and tell them not to expect her. She fumbled in her bag for the slip of paper with the number of the Hotel Quadro.

She gave the number to the telephone operator, who connected her with the operator at the Quadro.

"Bower? One moment, please." Kristin heard the phone ring once, twice, a dozen times. Then the operator came back on the line. "I'm sorry, Miss. There's no answer. Would you like to leave a message?"

Kristin, anxious to be on her way, said quickly, "I'm Kristin Mulroy. They were expecting me tonight, but I'm not coming down. I'm going to Haworth instead . . . well, never mind that. I only wanted to tell them I'm not coming."

She hung up and shrugged her shoulders. Another disappointment. She'd wanted to say goodbye to Alexa.

She looked at the clock. She had to hurry now if she expected to catch the bus to Haworth.

CHAPTER 11

"That's it up at the top of the hill," the taxi driver said. His thick Yorkshire accent reminded Kristin of a Scottish brogue. Of Richard's way of speaking.

Kristin, looking off at the giant, blue-misted moors in the distance, felt a twinge of pain as she remembered Richard. She forced herself to look away from the moors, to look up the steep cobble-stoned hill that was the main street of Haworth. Tourists thronged the narrow sidewalks; little Fiats and Fords and Volkswagens inched their way down the road's steep incline.

The Red Lion Inn was at the apex of a triangle formed by the main road branching into a fork — one road leading toward the moors, the other up the gently sloping countryside.

"They're fine people, the Whalleys. They run the inn, and they're sure to take good care of you." The taxi driver deposited Kristin's bag at the entrance and grinned widely when she tipped him. "Have a nice stay."

Inside, Kristin met Maurice Whalley, a tall, weatherbeaten Yorkshireman with a bantering air.

"Now here we've got a genuine Miss America!" he called to his wife as Kristin signed in. Peggy Whalley, his wife, was a cheerful, hardworking woman who — as Kristin was to learn — responded quickly and with wit to her husband's endless badgering.

"Don't pay him any mind," Peggy Whalley said, helping Kristin up the stairs with her bags. "Maurice is a good man and hardworking. I do think half the time he's wishing he was checking into somebody else's hotel — in America, I believe that's his preference."

"That would be wonderful," Kristin said. "When do you think you might go?"

"Oh, my dear, that's just one of life's dreams," the woman said pleasantly. "I'm afraid we'll never get there. We haven't the money nor the time to take away from here."

"You never know," Kristin said. "If you came to America, I'll bet my mother would love you both to stay with us."

The mention of her mother unexpectedly set off a stream of tears. Mrs. Whalley looked at her in astonishment.

"Well, my dear! What is it?" She came to Kristin's side.

"It — it's my mother," Kristin managed, wiping her eyes. "She — she's missing! And I can't find her anywhere. That's why I've come here."

She felt inconsolable; she tried to but could not control her grief. She sobbed and her shoulders shook violently. Mrs. Whalley put a motherly arm around her and led her to a small cretonne-covered loveseat by the window.

"Do you want to tell me about it?" Mrs. Whalley said. "You needn't if you don't want to." But her voice was warm, encouraging, not unlike her own mother's when there was a problem.

So Kristin started to speak. She told everything, and when she was finished, Peggy Whalley sat silent, brows lowered, for a few minutes. Then she spoke.

"I wouldn't be too upset, if I was you. Maurice and I have no children, but I can understand how you feel." She paused, then looked at Kristin directly. "Our country's different from yours — from all I've heard and read about America. We don't go about shooting and stabbing and kidnapping people here. It's not like us."

Kristin, encouraged by the woman's words, said, "But if that's so — and I believe it, I really do — then what in the world could have happened to my mother?"

Peggy Whalley studied her face a moment, as if looking for a hint of what to say. Then she shrugged her shoulders. "I think there's been a mixup in dates or places or some such thing . . ."

Kristin's heart sank. What was this woman trying to do? Make her think she was stupid, or crazy or something? Or did she have some motive in talking this way?

Kristin stood up. "It's very nice of you to take this trouble," she said. "But I guess it's a problem I'll have to work out on my own."

Peggy Whalley picked up the bags. "We'll talk another time. You're tired. Come on, I'll show you to your room, Kristin."

It was a very pleasant room, with a big bay window in front, overlooking the town.

"We'll have to ask you to give us the room back tomorrow night," Mrs. Whalley said. "You'll probably find a place at the Hillside Hotel for the night. Then you can come back and stay again, if you like. We've reserved it tomorrow for some rich Americans."

Kristin understood. The rich Americans were probably paying twice what she was. She couldn't blame Peggy Whalley. All the same, she felt uneasy. *I've made a mistake — telling her all I did. Maybe she's in with the kidnappers.*

Now where had that come from? *Kidnappers?* Why had she thought that? She shuddered, feeling it could be true. Either her mother was dead or some people were keeping her a prisoner. But if the latter — where? And for what reason? Certainly not for money. Then what?

She shook her head, went to the window, and looked out at the main street that dropped so steeply away from the inn. She saw a sign, FISH AND CHIPS, and mentally registered that she would go there for a meal. Her money was running low. She should have taken that money from Alexa. She opened her purse and counted its contents, and her heart stopped. All she had was seven pounds and some change. And her room was £6.95 a night. What was she thinking of? She had seen the sign downstairs: ALL ROOMS MUST BE PAID ON A DAILY BASIS. After she paid her bill that evening, she would be left with a few pence. And after that?

Life was closing in on her. She wanted to burst out in screams and flail her arms and pound the walls and go wild.

Again the feeling, *I'm in a dream; this isn't happening*, swept over her. She would lie down and take a nap.

She walked to the window and closed it. She drew the curtains together.

She did not see the man loitering in the street below, holding a tourist guidebook in his hand, but furtively stealing a look at the curtains closing in on the window.

When Kristin woke up, she was hungry, very hungry. She crossed to the sink, ran the water, and drank two glasses. The cool water filled her up, but she knew the feeling would not last long.

She took out her purse and counted her money again. She could possibly spare twenty-five pence — fifty cents — and that was it. Tomorrow she would have to move into the little inn the Whalleys had recommended. If they needed money in advance, she could not pay it and she would be disgraced, trying to cheat a local out of money.

What should she do next?

"Think — then act," her mother had said.

"I'll do it," she told herself in the mirror. "I'll worry about tomorrow — *tomorrow*. I've got a lot to catch up on."

She walked down the stairs and there was Mr. Whalley at the front desk.

"Well, and how's our American?" he asked pleasantly, his big face grinning. "How about a bit of food? Some sandwiches? Tea?"

Her stomach contracted as he spoke. What would he say if he knew she had no money to pay for anything except her room?

"Thank you — I'm not hungry just yet," she lied.

"Then I suppose you'll be doing a tour of the parsonage? And the Black Bull Inn? And the other Brontë highlights?" He seemed very interested as he awaited her reply.

"Oh, yes. I don't know if Mrs. Whalley told you about . . . about why I'm here," she began.

"Yes, she did," he said. "Peggy's got a great way with her, getting people to talk, hasn't she?" Then, quickly changing his tone, he said, "Now why don't you let us give you the grand tour? I could use a bit of air before tea, and I may as well drag along my old lady." This last he said with a grin as his wife came and overheard the conversation.

"So it's old that I am?" she countered. "Then what are you, I'd like to know — having seven years more than I."

"But I'm just a boy at heart," Maurice said.

"And a child in the brain," she retorted. She turned to Kristin. "Listen, my dear, Maurice is right about one thing. If you want to find out in a hurry what Haworth's all about, we're your people. Want us to show you around? Then you can get to do your own digging around tomorrow, at least knowing where you're going and what's what."

"I'd love it," Kristin said. "If it isn't too much trouble."

"Not a bit of it. We need a breather." Mrs. Whalley put her arm through Kristin's as her husband led the way out of the inn.

"Now, that's the Brontë parsonage up there," he said as they mounted the left fork of the cobblestone road outside. "That's the first thing to be seeing. It's where the Reverend Brontë raised his children after his wife died. Six children he had."

"Yes," his wife said. "And by the time young Charlotte was eight years old, two of them had already died. Her sisters Maria and Elizabeth got sick in the clergy children's school and were sent home to die of tuberculosis.

"And that left just Charlotte, Emily, and Anne Brontë and their brother Branwell."

"Charlotte Brontë wrote *Jane Eyre*," Kristin said. "And Emily wrote *Wuthering Heights*. I think Anne wrote something, too. But I never heard anything about the brother, Branwell."

"And thereby hangs quite a tale," Maurice said, smiling at her approvingly. "But come inside now, and watch your head as we go about. The Brontës, like many in those days, were small people."

They entered the tan brick building and walked into a large room to the left of the entrance. There the living room had been converted into a museum with showcases. In one showcase, Kristin saw notebooks, written in tiny, tiny handwriting. Some books were signed *Currer Bell.*

" 'Bell' is the name the Brontë sisters wrote under," Maurice Whalley said.

"They used to entertain themselves drawing pictures and making up stories," Peggy Whalley said. "They did a whole long adventure story, about the Glass People, a family they invented, and all the things that happened to them."

Now they were in the tiny sitting room, admiring the well-kept furniture, standing on the same old carpet the Brontës had trod. Among the paintings on the wall, a portrait of the Reverend Brontë, stern-faced, watched their every move.

"He looks very strict," Kristin said.

"That he was," Peggy Whalley said. "Which may well be the reason his son Branwell turned out so badly."

"What happened to Branwell?" Kristin asked, unable to hold her curiosity back.

"The poor boy tried his hand at painting, but he had no real gift for it. Come, here's a picture he did of his sister Charlotte." She led the way to the next room.

Kristin surveyed the portrait of Charlotte on the wall, and while the colors were attractive, even to her uncritical eye, the picture wasn't right. The features seemed slightly askew, and the execution of the oil paints looked amateurish.

"The father had high hopes for Branwell," Maurice said. "When his art career didn't work out, Branwell took to hanging out with a wild crowd, drinking and carousing."

"And more than drinking," his wife said. "He turned to drugs. They say he helped bring the drug business into Haworth through the underground —"

"Peggy! No point filling the girl's head with that rubbish!" Maurice Whalley's ruddy complexion was magenta now, and his happy-go-lucky manner was gone.

"I'm only trying to give her the information everyone knows, Maurice," Peggy Whalley retorted.

"If you'll come with me . . ." Maurice Whalley took Kristin's arm and walked her into a small gallery, where a bronze life-size sculpture of a young girl stood. It was Charlotte Brontë.

"Is this really supposed to be life-size?" Kristin asked. "Why, she's tiny!"

"Yes, she was," Peggy Whalley said. "Probably no more than four feet eight or nine. Like most of the Brontë children, except Branwell, she was delicate."

"*Charlotte Brontë, 1816–1855,*" Kristin read from the plaque at the base of the statue. "Why, she was only thirty-nine years old when she died."

"That's true. And world-famous. She had just married this preacher who'd been wanting to marry her for ten years. And they were happy together — so happy. And then she died in childbirth," Peggy Whalley said sadly. "Pity."

By this time Maurice Whalley had maneuvered them to the exit, where he again took charge.

"See that building yonder?" He indicated a dark graystone building with a brown shingled roof. "That's the Black Bull Inn — Branwell Brontë's hangout."

The next stop was Haworth Olde Hall, a handsome building that looked like the long-ago mansion of a very rich man, which indeed it had been.

The Whalleys took Kristin inside, showed her the lovely dining rooms, and introduced her to Peter Flange, the owner, who took great pride in announcing the various delights of the beautiful old building.

"History says, young lady, that during the Industrial Revolution, when the machines were coming in and putting knitters and other workers out of jobs, an underground network was set up to transmit messages and such," the owner said. "I don't suppose you Americans know about such things."

"But we do!" Kristin said. "During our Civil War, when the North was fighting to free the slaves in the South, many people helped slaves to run away." Kristin was happy to be able to give historical information about America to people like this, people whose lives were drenched in tradition. "As a matter of fact, many Southerners got involved and cooperated with the North to help the slaves escape. They formed what was called the underground railroad."

Maurice Whalley's face clouded. "You know full well, Peter, the underground tunnels haven't been used in decades."

"True." Mr. Flange pointed out a metal plaque on the wall to Kristin. "That grille over there is matched on the outside by another one that covers an entranceway to the old tunnel. People could get into the tunnel from outside as well as in here."

"Now stop with your stupid tales." Maurice Whalley was angry now. "This young lady shouldn't have to listen to such rubbish. She has no business with suchlike at all!"

The owner turned to Kristin. "Are you just a tourist then, young lady?"

Kristin said, "No. I'm here because I was to meet my mother in London last week, and she never arrived." She gulped. "The last I heard, she was traveling with a young blonde woman. I thought she might have visited here. She was very interested in the Brontës."

Peter Flange thought a moment. His eyes lit up. "Your mother. An American. About"— he surveyed Kristin —"say in her mid-forties somewhere?"

Kristin nodded energetically. "Yes, yes. Have you seen someone like her?"

"Yes. Yes, I did," Peter Flange said thoughtfully. "There was an American lady like that, brown hair, eyeglasses. She was here with a pretty girl who seemed British. Blonde hair. Very sweet and talked a lot during the lunch."

"When was this?" Kristin's heart beat so rapidly she had difficulty breathing. "When was this? It's very important! I've got to know!"

"Well, it seems to me it was Saturday lunch. Yes, that was it. I know because the lady — your mother — mentioned she was going to catch the afternoon train to London and she kept looking at her watch."

Kristin's hand went to her chest. She forced herself to slow down, to speak quietly. "What was she wearing? Can you remember?"

Peter Flange smiled at her. "It's my business to know such things. One notices clothing. Shoes are the giveaway, you know. Expensive shoes — people have money. Run down at the heel — that's another story."

Kristin listened patiently as he rambled on. Then he recollected himself and said, "Your mother, if that's who she was, was wearing a thin silk dress. Lavender, purple, whatever you call it —"

Kristin interrupted him. "Purple is my mother's favorite color! Half her clothes are in one shade or another of purple!"

"The young lady with her was very attractive. Very. At first I thought she was your age, but then after a good look, I'd say she was more in her late twenties. Early thirties, maybe."

Maurice Whalley said, "I hope you've got what you want. We have to be getting back to the inn."

A few minutes later they were making their way up the steep cobblestone road toward the Red Lion Inn. On the way, they passed an old, rather run-down hotel with a sign in front, HILLSIDE HOTEL. There was a little bookshop in the front on the first floor.

"That's where you can stay tomorrow night,"

Peggy Whalley said. "It's old, but comfortable. And it's half the price of our place."

When they got to the top of the hill, the Whalleys said they had to go. "I'm sorry indeed we couldn't take you into the Black Bull Inn," Maurice Whalley said.

"Won't you come in and have some tea with us?" Mrs. Whalley said.

Kristin, famished by now, was tempted. Perhaps they meant to treat her. She didn't know. If not, she would be in the impossible position of having it on her bill and being unable to pay.

"Thanks, no," she said. She could hear the rumbling of her stomach. She had eaten no dinner last night — what with Richard running off and leaving her alone in the Chinese restaurant. And her breakfast at the inn in Chester had been toast and tea.

In her entire life she had never known real hunger for more than a couple of hours. Now she looked longingly in on the bakeshops they were passing, wondering if they had anything for as little as twenty-five pence. If she had that much.

When she awoke, she saw a dark gray day outside. She looked at her watch, and was shocked to see the time. Two o'clock in the afternoon! She had slept almost around the clock! Unbelievable. Physical and emotional exhaustion had wiped her out completely.

She was aware of the gnawing feeling of hunger in her stomach, but she bathed and hastily packed her bag. It was three o'clock when she went downstairs to check out.

Neither of the Whalleys was there, but a young man in a blue porter's outfit took out her bill, looked it over, and said, "You're all paid up, Miss. Don't owe a thing."

She nodded, relieved. "Thank you. I'll be on my way."

"Give you a hand, Miss?"

"No, thank you." She picked up her bag and walked out.

What now?

With so little money, she could hardly go anywhere in town. She would have liked to go to the Black Bull Inn — it had looked so cozy — but she could hardly be welcome to sit around there and order nothing.

The sky had begun to darken. *I must find shelter for the night.*

She looked toward the moors and thought, *Maybe there's some place up there.*

She really had no alternative. She could not wander the town until nightfall, and after that it would be even worse. She clutched her bag, slung her tote bag over her shoulder, started up the right-hand fork that led to the foot of the moors.

As she trudged uphill she felt her hunger acutely.

How did poor people manage to survive, penniless? They often went to sleep hungry. How did homeless people get through from one day to the next? Well, she'd have a taste of it now. She would not, could not, leave Haworth without searching further. And if she had no money, it was her hard luck. She had managed badly. It was up to her to carry on as best she could if she hoped to find her mother.

She reached the narrow, dusty road that led to the moors. The leaden skies overhead were full of rain clouds now and she felt the first clear, cold drops on her face, on her hair. She hurried along, for the rain was quickly changing from a light sprinkle to a heavy downpour.

She stayed on the narrow path, bordered on either side with furze and other low-lying foliage. The path took her up to the top of a hillock. From there she could look down on the far side of the moors.

The panoramic view held her spellbound. A faint blue haze hung over the valleys and the farmland. Sheep, gray as the dusty roads leading up, with faces and forelocks black as the loam that lay in rows on the moors, grazed aimlessly. She saw a waterfall a short distance below. She had to follow a narrow footpath that turned out to be a well-worn route for the goats and some cows.

The harsh bleat of a goat frightened her. The path narrowed and became moist and then muddy. Soon she had to step from slippery rock to rock to keep going.

The rain was coming down hard now. She *had* to find someplace dry, someplace safe. She saw beside a waterfall an overhanging rock that managed to form a small cave, with walls made of boughs and dirt and a hard dirt floor underfoot.

She looked inside hesitantly. There were some empty beer cans and paper wrappers from snacks and candy bars. They looked like they had been there a long time. She put her bag down inside and sat on it, feeling faint with hunger.

She heard the waterfall nearby, and suddenly she got up and left the cave and made her way in the downpour to where the waterfall ran along some rocks on its downhill rush, forming little pools. She cupped her hands and scooped up handful after handful of the cold, rushing water.

Her stomach contracted and she felt the beginning of cramps. The cold water chilled her and she started to shake. She hurried back to the little cave, but a few feet away she saw some small red berries on a bush. Two birds were perched beneath a branch, pecking away at the berries.

I wonder if it's all right for me to eat some of those berries? If they were poison, the birds couldn't be eating them. She knew how foolhardy it was to take a chance, but she reached out and plucked a berry from a branch, ruffling the bush and causing the birds to fly off in fright. She bit into the small red berry and let just a drop or two of its juice into her mouth. It was delicious — sweet and mild. But then she was frightened. Maybe there were poisons that tasted like this.

How did I ever get into this nightmare? What will I do tomorrow? What will happen to me tonight? Maybe there are wild animals up here on the moors. Or snakes.

She was terribly tired now. She went back into the cave and sat down on the suitcase again.

It was still light enough out for her to read. She reached into her tote bag and picked up the mangled copy of *Jane Eyre* that the clerk at Chester had given her. She opened the book at random and started to read.

Incredibly, her eyes found the lines:

> And I sank down where I stood, and hid my face against the ground. I lay still a while: the night-wind swept over the hill and over me, and died moaning in the distance; the rain fell fast, wetting me afresh to the skin.

She was in the same situation as Jane Eyre! She was hungry, wet, cold, suffering in a way she had never known before. But Jane Eyre's predicament had been worse than her own. Kristin *did* have friends in the world she could call on (*had* called on — the Bowers — and where were they?). She could probably throw herself on the mercy of the Whalleys, or the police, or even friendly townspeople, but it was so debasing to do that. And how was she to know a friend from someone who might have private interests — interests that might be injurious to her mother, wherever she was?

Avidly, she read the book and, strangely, found strength in it. Yes, it was fiction, but the book and the character of Jane had come from Charlotte Brontë's soul, her self. It was not a persona, an image, but a projection of a real person.

I will be strong. I will overcome. I will find my mother.

But suddenly night was falling, and strange

noises and strange creatures were creeping over the moors. Her body was racked with cold, her hunger was overpowering. She reached outside the cave and pulled up a clump of grass and started to chew it. She opened her suitcase, took out a woolen jacket, and spread it on the ground. A profound sense of exhaustion crept over her and she fell sound asleep, while outside the mouth of the cave, the rain roared down in the blackness of the night.

Margaret Clark lay there in the dark, listening to the rain pounding down somewhere above, outside the thick stone walls. Dampness throughout the room where she lay on the cold floor invaded her entire body. The candle Pamela had left had gone out. Nearby she heard the tiny squeaks and hurrying taps of rodent feet on the stone floor and walls. She shivered; her blood ran cold as she realized how little strength she had left.

"Oh, God!" she cried. "I can't last much longer. I truly can't."

CHAPTER 12

The screech of an owl was the first sound that Kristin heard. The rain was still coming down in a flood and the little cave had not protected her very well. She was drenched to the bone and cold, so cold she awoke trembling. Her lips were blue and her hands and feet were numb.

Cramped, aching in her joints, Kristin arose and looked through the curtain of rain at the sodden hillside. She had to get out of there. What she needed more than anything was a place that was dry and warm, a change of clothes, and food. Her stomach was one persistent ache, her hunger gnawed at her vitals.

She took a plastic bag out of her suitcase, covered her hair with it, and anchored it with a couple of bobby pins.

As she was about to leave the cave, something made her look up and off to the very tip of the moor. There she saw the silhouette of the stone building that the Whalleys had shown her in the map on the hotel wall. She remembered the name now. Top Withens. The place where Emily

Brontë was supposed to have set the scene for her book *Wuthering Heights.*

A fever of curiosity seized her. *I'll go there. I've got to see for myself.* What it was that she hoped to find there she did not know, but her feeling was as strong, as real, as if something tangible were pulling her there.

But I can't take all this with me. She put the suitcase down, took her hairbrush, her tourist guide, and a few other heavy items from her tote bag and placed them beside the suitcase. She took out a woolen plaid cape and slipped it around her shoulders.

Then, tightening the plastic bag around her hair, she started the long, steep climb up the side of the moor. There was no one — nothing — out there in the rain. Even the animals were gone. Several times she slipped on the damp earth, but each time she managed to regain her footing.

It seemed an endless journey. Her clothes were damp and stuck to her skin. She was terribly hungry and her body ached in every joint. But she would not stop. She had to keep on.

Once or twice she got the feeling that she was being followed. She turned and looked about nervously but each time saw nothing. Why did she have this strong sense that she was being watched? Maybe it was her hunger. *I've read about people starving. Sometimes they begin to imagine things. I must be imagining someone is here.* Only a crazy person would be wandering in a place like this on a day like this. There's nothing here but that building way up the moors.

Why should I go there? She knew it was unreasonable, but she kept stubbornly on. She had never in her life dreamed of such punishment as her body was undergoing now. But above the strain of climbing the jagged side of the moor, above the constant stabbing pangs of hunger, above the dizziness she felt as she walked ever upward, always there was this urgency to reach the top, to get to that building, whatever the cost.

All time seemed to have stopped. How long had she been climbing the hillside? The blackened sky gave no hint. It could be six o'clock in the morning or closer to noon. But time didn't matter. She would keep on going until she reached the top or dropped.

She trod desperately on, head lowered against the rain. But then, when at last she raised her eyes from the treacherous ground beneath her feet, she saw the house only yards away! The ancient, windswept ruin — Top Withens.

There was no door to bar her way. She stood in front of the gaping hole that was the entrance and surveyed the remains of what had once been a warm, beautiful home, a comfort for people now long dead. It was dramatic evidence of humanity laid waste, ravaged testimony to the brevity of human life on this earth. The house atop the gigantic crouching moor was a timeless reminder that the land had a life of its own, outlasting the centuries. The moor had been there for ages untold.

Shivering with cold, Kristin drew her cape

closer around her, stepped on the stone stoop, and entered the house.

The wind whined through windows from which glass panes had long ago been ripped; now there were only long, rotted, wooden frames and yawning holes. It was dark inside the building. The windows were tiny, while the low ceilings and stone walls would have kept the rooms dark on even the sunniest of days.

Kristin walked tentatively from one small room to another. Once she thought she heard a voice. She stopped dead in her tracks, but though she waited anxiously, no sound came. There was only the crack of bushes slapping against the house and the wind howling around the corner.

That must be what I heard. The wind. I can't stay here forever. It's freezing. I'll get sick if I do.

All of a sudden a wave of surrender swept through her. *I'm an idiot. This is all stupid.* She was so disgusted with herself she became sick to her stomach, and the dreadful feeling swept through her, down her arms, her legs. She felt as if she was choking. She had no way of knowing that her weakness and irresolution were symptoms of acute hunger. Her judgment was blurred; she did not see things as they were. Her knees suddenly sagged beneath her and she had to grab a wooden slat on the wall beside her for support. As she did, the slat moved, askew, revealing a cupboard, hoary with age and filth. There was a squeak, and a thin, dark gray rat stood glaring at her with red eyes. She screamed and ran through the doorway and kept running, down, down the hillside, half-sliding, half-falling. Gone was her exhaustion. The adrenaline in her body gave her a strength she had not felt for almost two days. But even that false courage deserted her by the time she neared the cave.

When she reached the cave, she was gasping for breath. Inside, she leaned against the dirt wall to gather strength to go on. She looked longingly at the dry dirt floor and thought how wonderful it would be just to lie down and sleep. But some instinct for survival nagged at her, would not let her quit.

She swayed weakly as she picked up her bag and summoned up every ounce of determination to carry it outside. Her head was spinning again and her legs trembled from weakness as she left the dry, quiet, little cave that had given her sanctuary through the long, stormy night.

The moors were deserted. The heavy downpour had discouraged even the most ardent tourist. Here and there she heard the mournful cry of an occasional goat trying to make its way homeward in the storm.

The road to town seemed miles away, but she gritted her teeth and stumbled down the path she had struggled up so painfully the day before. The suitcase was a staggering burden; its weight dragged her faster down the wet, slippery hillside than her normal pace. Her mind was full of strange, vague thoughts; her vision was blurred — whether from the rain or from her weakened physical condition, she could not tell.

Then all at once, her strength ebbing fast, she

looked down and saw the road that led back to Haworth. With a monumental effort, she made it to the hard cement road.

Who would take in anyone looking as she did? Her clothes were wet, her hair a mass of tangles under the strange little piece of plastic. She was pale and starving and felt feverish. *I've got to keep on.* She gritted her teeth and slogged along the road, the weight of her suitcase dragging behind her. One or two cars passed her, going in the opposite direction. If the drivers looked at her, she could not have known; the rain was heavy on their windshields.

Now she was coming to the main street. She slunk alongside the Red Lion Inn and saw no one from there. A few people, in raincoats and carrying umbrellas, were hurrying along the street, but no one paid any attention to her, nor she to them.

On an impulse she looked up and saw the battered old sign of the Hillside Hotel. It was creaking in the wind and the rain, and on an impulse she walked up the three wooden steps to the entrance, where a sign said, WELCOME.

She opened the door slowly and peered inside. She saw a small room, shabby carpets, chipped wooden chairs, ragged upholstered sofa. In the rear of the room there was a television set going and no one watching it.

On a small table near the door there was a small push bell with a sign in front of it, RING BELL FOR SERVICE. Somewhere in the building, food was cooking. Kristin smelled bacon and coffee and freshly baked bread. The scent of the food set her senses whirling. She felt dizzy and seized the edge of a table for support just as a woman entered the room. Kristin saw her through a haze. She was short and stocky, and she said in that slightly gruff Yorkshire manner, "Yes? Is there something you want?"

Then she took a better look at Kristin. She saw the dripping hair, the wet clothing, and she looked askance at a puddle that was forming on the floor where Kristin had set her things down.

"What is it? What do you want, Miss?" This time her voice was harsher.

Kristin passed a hand over her forehead, thinking, *I look awful. I can't ask her for anything. I have no money.*

She said, "Nothing," but no sound came; her throat was locked. She tried again. "Thank you, nothing." This time it was little better than a whisper. Kristin picked up her luggage and went to the door.

"Are you all right?" the woman said.

Kristin nodded and turned the doorknob. Outside, the rain was coming down harder than ever. Water dripping on her face, in her eyes, she stood irresolute on the top of the steps, her legs unsteady, feeling too weak to hold the iron railing. She was on the brink of unconsciousness when she heard the voice.

"Kristin!"

It was a voice from a dream. A familiar voice. She swayed on the top step and might have fallen, but someone seized her in strong arms and said, "Kristin!" and it was Alexa.

"Kristin, darling, what's the matter?" Alexa took Kristin gently and turned her around. Kristin looked dully at her friend and let herself be led back into the Hillside Hotel.

Inside, Alexa helped her over to a sofa and set her down carefully. Her anxious eyes searched her friend's face carefully.

"Kristin! Are you sick?"

Kristin's eyes filled with tears. She touched Alexa's hand weakly and said, "Not . . . sick. No . . . food . . ."

The short, stocky woman entered the front room again. She started to speak but Alexa cut her off.

"Do you serve food here?"

The woman nodded. "Well, of course we do. Is it a meal you're wanting?"

"That's right. Please bring something right away. My friend isn't feeling well." She opened her purse and let the woman see the thick roll of bills in her wallet. "What have you got?"

The woman spoke more respectfully now. "Well, if the young lady is feeling poorly, I have a fine broth rich with meat and barley that will pick her up."

Alexa said, "Yes, yes. That will be very nice. And bring some toast or crackers with it, please."

The woman hurried off and Alexa bent over Kristin, who was lying with her head back on the shabby velvet sofa, her eyes closed.

"Is that all right, Kris? I mean, the soup?" Kristin, eyes still closed, nodded ever so lightly.

Alexa, seeing her friend's wet clothing, said, "Just lie there, Kris." Then she thought, *As if the poor thing could do anything else.* She opened Kristin's suitcase and pulled out a cotton robe, wrinkled, but dry. She started to unbutton Kristin's sweater when the woman reentered the room.

"She's soaked. Is it all right if I put something dry on her?" Alexa asked.

"Do it and don't delay. There's always the danger of a bad cold or bronchitis or worse." The woman took another look at Kristin's dead-white face. "I'll fetch some nice dry towels," she said.

The woman and Alexa seemed to have an unspoken agreement that Kristin must not be moved, that she was too weak, and that neither of them knew how Kristin had come to such a sorry state.

In a minute the woman was back with a huge flannel robe and several towels. "Here, dear, wrap her in this." She handed the big towel over. "And dry her with these. I'll fetch the broth."

Again she bustled out. In the few minutes she was gone, Alexa took off Kristin's wet shoes and clothing, rubbed her down, and got her into the warm dry robe.

Kristin, too weak to help, let herself be handled like a limp rag doll. Once she tried to smile at Alexa but her mouth fell slack. It was only when the woman returned with a steaming bowl of broth and the wonderful aroma reached her nostrils that Kristin opened her eyes.

Alexa brought a spoonful to Kristin's lips and said, "Take it slowly, Kristin. Easy does it."

The taste of that first spoonful was paradise. She had never in her life known food could taste like this. Tears of weakness ran slowly down her cheek, her face turned pink again, and her eyes were open now. After half the soup had been spooned into her mouth, she smiled.

"You're wonderful," she whispered.

"Traveling around without any money," Alexa said accusingly. "You must be starved. How long since the last time you ate?"

Kristin said, "Don't remember . . . too long."

"It's a wonderful way to diet," Alexa said, "if you don't die doing it."

By this time Kristin had finished the bowl of soup and was feeling incredibly better. The nightmare of the past three days was over. Dear Alexa was here. She had to tell her everything. But she was too weak to talk much. She did tell about getting sick in Chester.

"I knew you should have come back to London with me," Alexa said indignantly. "We'll go back tomorrow, or whenever you're strong enough."

"No. I can't go back. I can't stop. Not now." Her eyes welled up again.

"Don't get excited, Kristin. It's okay." Alexa looked around the dingy little waiting room. "This isn't Buckingham Palace —" she began.

As if on cue the woman returned. She surveyed the empty soup bowl, saw Kristin munching on a biscuit, saw the new look of awareness on her face. She was pleased.

"Well, I see that you're feeling much better."

"Could we rent a room?" Alexa asked. "For just a few days?"

"It's the height of the season, but I think we can put you up," she said.

Kristin said happily, "Thank you." She would have said more, but she felt weak; her head started to loll back again.

"Have you got a room where she won't have to walk the stairs?" Alexa said.

The woman picked up the luggage and said, all business again, "Follow me."

It was a small room in the rear looking out directly on the moors. There was a double bed and a small cot. Kristin was helped into the big bed and covered with clean sheets and a warm wool blanket and the inevitable puffed comforter. Before all the covers were on her, she was sound asleep.

She woke up once and was fed again, this time nourishing solid food. And then she dropped off once more. All in all, she slept for almost thirty-six hours. This time when she awoke it was Thursday noon.

"I don't believe it," she said, stretching luxuriously. The weather was still gray outside, but in the little room a lamp was burning brightly and Alexa sat beside the bed surveying Kristin with pleasure.

"Now, tell me all," Alexa demanded.

"No, *you* tell me. How did you find me? What made you come to Haworth?"

"You phoned our hotel, didn't you?"

"Yes, but you weren't there."

"But I was. Mother and Dad were off with dear Aunt Betty, and I had a headache so I stayed behind." She shook her head. "The operator must have rung the wrong room."

"I still don't know how you found me." Kristin sat up against the pillows.

"The operator said someone named Kristin had phoned and said she wasn't coming, but said something about going to Haworth. We were very upset by that. So the three of us had a big conference. My folks said I should come up to Haworth, find you and bring you back. The man at the Red Lion Inn told me he thought you were still someplace in town. He sent me here."

That reminded Kristin. All the anxiety, the misery, of her mother's disappearance swept back in a monumental cloud, sending her back into the deepest depression.

Alexa saw the change come over Kristin and thought hopelessly, *What's the use? Her mother must be dead by now.*

She tried to hide her feelings, not very successfully, as Kristin threw back the covers and swung her legs over the side of the bed.

"Take it easy," Alexa said. "You're still as weak as a fish. A weakfish, get it?"

"Don't bother, Alexa. I'll be careful, I promise, but let's go into town and see what we can find. I'm going to get dressed."

"You're not up to it," Alexa said, trying to sound authoritative.

"I can't stay here and do nothing. Don't try to stop me." There was a strange glitter in Kristin's eyes.

CHAPTER 13

"Did you have a Dr. Margaret Clark staying here last week?" Kristin asked the man behind the desk in the Black Bull Inn.

"I'm sorry, Miss," the man said apologetically. "The books are locked up right now. If you come round in the morning —" He stopped. "It does sound familiar, that name. I believe she was here one night. With another lady. I'm fairly certain it was this weekend past."

"Can't you get the books sooner than tomorrow morning?" Kristin said, excited and impatient.

"I'm afraid not, Miss. The owner locks his records in the safe overnight, and none but he knows how to open it." The clerk shook his head sympathetically. "Sorry I can't help."

"Come on," Alexa said, taking Kristin's arm. "We'll come back in the morning."

Kristin stood there undecided. The handsome old inn was bustling. It was five o'clock, the end of the work day, and the crowd inside was a happy, boisterous one.

As the two girls walked slowly away from the desk, two young men detached themselves from a group at the bar and came toward them. One boy was tall and slim and well built and as handsome as a male model back in the States. The other was short, no more than five-six, and rather plump; his uneven features and unruly hair made him almost a comic figure.

It was the short one who spoke first. "I say, need some help?" He smiled and his irregular face looked lopsided. "By the bye, my name is Alfie Crewes" — he indicated the tall silent young man beside him — "and this chap is Matthew Rosebury." Again that crooked smile appeared.

"I'm Alexa Bower," Alexa said brightly, "and this is my best friend, Kristin Mulroy." Then she hurried on to say, "And we'd love some help." She beamed at the tall one, Matthew, and he flushed.

"I say," Alfie said, "why don't we have a seat and chat a bit?"

Kristin looked around at the crowded barroom and the laughing people and said, "Thank you, it's very nice of you, but I'm a little tired, and it's very close in here." She started for the door. "Are you coming, Alexa?"

"Why don't you come with us?" Alexa said to Alfie. Then she smiled at Matthew. "I've heard so much about the moors of Yorkshire, and I've never set foot on one. Is it too late to take a walk up there now?"

"Not at all," Alfie answered for his friend. "It's only minutes from here. Matter of fact, Matthew and I want to have a look at old man Harrington's new black-faced sheep. Right, Matthew?"

Matthew said, "Right."

"Is that the help you wanted?" Alfie asked. "To see the moors?"

"No," Kristin said, as Alexa said, "Yes."

The boys looked at them oddly. "Well, there's a fine sunset," Alfie said. "If we hurry, you'll see something rare, I promise you."

Without further conversation, they started up the hill toward the moors. The sun was now ablaze in a twilight glow; the scenery was breathtaking.

"Let's hurry," Alexa said. "I'd love to see that gorgeous sunset from the moors!"

But by the time they got to the top of the first hill, Alexa looked anxiously at Kristin, who was out of breath, and said to the two boys, "I don't think we should go any further. We can enjoy the sunset just as well from here."

Alfie gave Matthew a knowing look. He said, "Then it's fine with us. Why don't you two lassies stay here while we hurry on and have a quick look at Harrington's flock. Does that suit you?"

"Go right ahead," Alexa said. "We'll be perfectly fine right here."

But they were not fated to be perfectly fine. The two boys had no sooner reached the very crest of the moors than the sun dropped in the sky and a mass of heavy black clouds appeared out of nowhere. In moments, thunder rolled and bursts of blue electricity lit up the sky, and Alexa and Kristin felt the first few heavy raindrops. They ran for shelter.

"Not there!" Kristin yelled as Alexa stopped beneath a tree. "That's the first place lightning might strike!"

"Then where?" Alexa yelled back. "We'll get soaked!"

Kristin pointed to a low-hanging cliff that formed a shelter, not too unlike the cave in which she had spent that long, dreadful night right near here.

Once inside the small cave, both looked at each other's dripping hair and clothes and burst into laughter.

"I wonder where our boyfriends are," Alexa said, giggling.

"Alfie and Matthew?" Kristin flung an arm in the direction of the moor's crest. "Probably they're over yonder, getting the full blast . . . Oh, no!"

"What is it?" Alexa followed Kristin's pointing finger and saw what had transfixed her.

Against the bright blue flare of distant lightning, a wild, witchlike form was silhouetted with terrifying clarity. As they watched, the witch — for so it seemed to be — threw her head back and shouted at the sky. They could not hear what the wild woman was screaming, but they were shocked by her madness as she bent backward and shook her fists at the heavens. The two friends clasped each other in terror while the madwoman on the moors did a crazy little dance, threw her head back, cried out one last time at the sky, then disappeared.

"I don't believe it!" Alexa said. "It was a *witch*, Kristin!"

"Don't be ridiculous," Kristin said. "There are no witches."

"Then what was it?" Alexa demanded.

Kristin shook her head. "I don't know. Why would anyone be up here in a storm like this? She's crazy. Of course she is. Do you think the boys saw her?"

"Speaking of which," Alexa said, "where do you think the dear boys are? Do you suppose they've deserted us?"

"Could be . . ." Kristin said, looking out. "Listen, the rain is letting up. I'd rather get a little wetter going back to town than staying here with a maniac like that one" — she nodded her head toward where the witch-woman had disappeared — "hanging around and maybe even coming back."

"What are we waiting for?" Alexa grabbed her by the arm. "Let's head for town and get into some dry clothes before you get sick."

"What I can't figure out," Kristin said, letting herself be led down the slippery ground, "is where did Alfie and Matthew go? Did they leave us up here on purpose?"

Twenty minutes later they were back in town and passing the Black Bull Inn when the door was flung open and they saw Alfie and Matthew.

"What happened to you? We looked all over the bloomin' moors and couldn't find you," Alfie said.

"Come on in." Matthew motioned them inside. It was probably this unaccustomed friendliness of Matthew's that made Alexa and Kristin accept their invitation.

Inside, Alfie wasted no time. He took Kristin by the arm and said, "You're terribly serious. Never a smile since the moment we laid eyes on you." He spun her toward him and said, "Now tell Uncle Alfie. What's wrong? What's upsetting that pretty face of yours?"

Kristin was silent. Alexa said, "Do you two boys live in Haworth?" When they nodded, she said, "Then I think you can give us a hand." Her eyes pleaded with Kristin. "Listen, Kris, let's tell them about what we saw during the storm."

Kristin shrugged her shoulders. Turning back to the boys, Alexa told them of the strange wild woman and her fantastic behavior. "It was right out of a horror movie." Alexa shivered as she recalled the weird scene.

Alfie and Matthew exchanged glances. Then, as usual, Alfie spoke first. "We've heard stories every now and then about a wild woman that roams the moors. But it's been a long time since anyone claimed to see the witch — if there is such a creature." Matthew nodded agreement. "You didn't imagine it?"

"Alfie!" Alexa said indignantly. "We know what we saw and no one can talk us out of it."

"Well, don't get the old blood pressure up," Alfie said. "It still doesn't answer why Kristin's in the dumps, now does it?"

Instantly, Kristin's eyes commanded her to be

still, but Alexa ignored her. She started spouting information recklessly, information Kristin would have wanted to keep secret.

". . . so what we're doing here isn't simply acting like tourists. Haworth is a gorgeous town, but you see we're actually looking for —"

This time Kristin stopped her. "Alexa! For heaven's sake! You know I don't want to bother people with my problem. Please, let it go at that."

But Alfie, his brown eyes sparkling with recognition, broke in. "I say! You must be the American who's looking for that lady. Professor something or other. Am I right?"

Kristin could have happily throttled Alexa. She tried to be calm. "I am looking for someone. My — my mother. It's not too important, really. We've, uh, missed connections." She gave another warning look to Alexa, who paid no attention.

"Actually, we're very worried about Professor Clark, Kristin's mother," Alexa hurried on. "And we're trying to find out whether anyone saw her in Haworth."

Kristin looked suspiciously at Alfie. "How did you hear about us?"

"Oh, you don't keep secrets in a small place like Haworth. It was Maurice Whalley who happened to mention it." Then, seeing Kristin's look of distress, he said, "Now there, Kristin, don't take on so. This is a good town, with good people in it."

Alexa said, "You could give us a hand, Alfie." To Kristin she said, "Don't try to stop me. If these boys are from Haworth, we can find out that much quicker when your mother was here and when she left — if she left."

Again Alfie took matters in hand. Seizing Kristin by the arm, he led her to a small oak table with a huge wood-backed leather chair behind it and three small wooden chairs in front. "Have a seat," he said. Alexa and Matthew followed them and sat down. "Here, here," Alfie said, pounding a small push bell that was nailed to the table. "Let's have something to drink. That will cheer us up one, two, three."

Within minutes a waiter was bringing four pints of cider to the table and Alexa, ignoring Kristin's warning foot on hers under the table, said, "She's all upset. And so would you be. Her mother has been missing for almost a week."

Kristin sighed. "All right," she said, and went on to tell the whole story.

"I get it," Alfie said eagerly. "What you want is to find out if your mother was seen, with or without that young woman, someplace in town?" His brown eyes solemnly registered Kristin's assent. "And you want to know if anyone saw them leave town?"

Despite herself, Kristin found Alfie's persistence reassuring. "That's it. The man at Haworth Olde Hall said he saw someone that could have been my mother and the blonde woman was with her, and he said that . . ." She paused and then the memory of Peter Flange's words came back to her. "It's the metal grille outside the building — it leads to the underground tunnel — that I forgot about. Mr. Whalley got all upset when Mr. Flange mentioned it."

Alfie's face with its pudding features seemed to firm up before their eyes. "Listen, what we should do is have a look down there. Far as I know, no one has been down in those tunnels for ages." He scratched his nose thoughtfully. "We could have a go at it tonight, but it would have to be much later, when the Olde Hall settles down for the night."

"I don't think Kristin is up to any exploring tonight," Alexa began.

"Oh, yes, I am," Kristin said. "Please, let's do it tonight!"

"Then all right," Alfie said. "It's done!"

The boys walked them back to the Hillside Hotel. With a cheery, "Meet you at the Black Bull at eleven o'clock tonight," from Alfie, they were gone.

But as Alexa opened the front door, Kristin stopped her. "I don't feel like going in yet, Alexa. Do you mind if I hang out a while? The rain's stopped and I really feel all right. Honestly."

After a long look at her, Alexa said, "Go ahead, Kris. But don't be too long. It's very damp out, and you need your sleep."

Kristin squeezed Alexa's hand appreciatively and started back up the cobblestone street. She passed the Black Bull and made her way to the Brontë parsonage, a short distance away. She went into the grounds and found a fairly dry spot on a stone bench under a heavy oak tree. She sat down, pulling her cape closer around her. Out in the street she could hear the voices of people passing by, but here in the secluded yard she was completely alone. She looked out toward the moors, saw the huge lonely mountain with a faint silver haze over it, and her heart thudded miserably. *Oh God,* she thought. *Why am I here? What are we looking for? It's been six long days and there's not a sign of her.*

She sighed and her breath caught in her throat. *She's dead.*

Tears came, flooding her eyes, choking her. She could not stop. She dropped her face into her hands and gave vent to her sorrow, until she felt she could cry no more. She drew her hands away from her face and looked up to see, through the haze of tears, a figure standing there, directly in front of her.

Richard!

In a moment he had seized her by the arms and drawn her to him. She yielded completely to the incredible sensation of warmth and relief, standing there, being held by this formidable man who was now letting her cry in his arms, patting her gently and murmuring small words of comfort. "Go ahead and cry, Kristin. It's all right. I've been looking for you."

She looked up to see his brown eyes warm with an emotion beyond sympathy or pity. Those eyes were asking her a question and she lifted her face to his and in an instant their lips were pressed tightly against each other's. Her heart thrilled to his embrace. His kiss was a thousand times more exciting than she remembered.

"Oh, Kristin, if you only knew . . ." His voice against her cheek was husky, his warm breath a caress.

Then Richard said huskily, "I'm sorry, Kristin. It isn't fair to take advantage — you've got so much to bear as it is."

Kristin stiffened. Was he going to turn away again? She could not deal with another rejection by him. She started to pull away.

He said, "Kristin, I know I've given you no reason to trust me, none at all. But I've got to ask you to believe in me." When she looked at him coolly, he added, "I came up to Haworth looking for you. And that isn't all, believe me. I know the agony you're going through . . ." He shook his head as she silently waited. "Ah, what's the use? Let me take you back to where you're staying — the Hillside Hotel . . ." *How did he know?* ". . . ah, that's it. Come here now." He drew her close and kissed her once more on the lips. *Thank you for nothing*, she thought. *You're crazy, do you know that?* She hated herself for having responded to him so completely. *But that's just feeling*, she told herself. *In my head I know there's something wrong with him, terribly wrong. He's not for me. Not now or ever*. She didn't have the strength to verbalize any of this. Tomorrow, another day, it didn't matter. There was time enough.

At her door, Richard said, "Let's meet for lunch tomorrow?" As she said nothing, he added,

"Then lunch it is, at the Red Lion. I'll pick you up here at twelve-thirty. That all right?" Then she ducked her head slightly. "All right then," he said and walked briskly off down the cobblestone street, a tall figure, head and shoulders above the few late night strollers.

"Give him a chance," Alexa said. "Why don't you trust him, just once?"

"He's bad news," Kristin said. "I don't want to even think about him, Alexa." She looked at her watch. "In two more hours we're meeting Alfie and Matthew and they'll take us to that place. I want to go there more than anything!"

Privately, Alexa thought, *Poor kid. She's whistling in the dark. But I'll humor her. Anything to keep her from slipping back into that depression again.* Then, for the first time, she thought, *My God, I wonder what Kristin will do if — no, when — we find out her mother is dead.* The chilling thought sliced through her mind: *She's liable to do anything.*

Alexa couldn't wait for eleven o'clock. One way or the other, she and Kristin both knew tonight was the end of the road.

She awoke to the painful throbbing in her leg. She lay on the hard floor with her leg outstretched. The filthy, torn quilt beneath her was small protection from the cold, unyielding cement floor. Beside her, a bowl of some kind of thick meat soup rested on crumpled sheets of news-

paper. Next to that was a jar of water. She reached with difficulty for the jar and forced herself to drink the warm, rancid-tasting water. Her tongue felt on fire, her head burned with fever, yet she shivered in the dankness of the small dark room. The one tiny window high on the stone wall was obscured by bushes or trees from outside. By day she sometimes saw a small glimmer of light, but as the sun set the entire room was plunged into a frightening darkness.

She reached for the bowl of soup, took up the stained tin spoon, and forced herself to swallow some. It was filled with barely cooked lumps of potato, but she made herself eat the sour broth, lumps and all. She knew from the pain in her leg that the infection was getting worse. Possibly gangrene. If not now, then soon. She had to keep her strength up. If anyone could find her, let it be now. The Bowers would help. The British police force was famous for its efficiency. They would find a way to locate her. They would trace her down from the first moment she had left Edinburgh with Pamela.

Pamela. The madwoman. Even as Margaret Clark tried to comfort herself with these thoughts, she knew that Pamela, in her brilliant madness, had method enough to have left no traces behind them.

No one could possibly know where she was. And if and when someone finally figured it out — a week, two weeks? — it would be far too late. She touched the swollen, throbbing leg, and tears of weakness rose to her eyes. Then she drifted into unconsciousness again. Was it sleep? Unconsciousness? How long had she been here? A day, two, four, a week? Time no longer had meaning for her. Her last conscious thought was of Kristin. Kristin, who would have to make her way in the world alone.

Oh, hurry.

CHAPTER 14

"Well, you ladies are right on time. What a surprise," Alfie said as the four met outside the Black Bull Inn.

"Come off it," Alexa said, punching Alfie's arm lightly. "That's a lot of old superstition — women are late, women can't make up their minds, women are afraid of the dark —"

At that moment, something swift and light brushed against her legs and Alexa let out a small shriek.

"Superstition?" Alfie said, laughing. "That was only a town cat passing by and Miss America is ready to fall into a faint." He twinkled at Kristin. "Isn't that so, Kristin?" He saw that her mind was miles away. "Kristin?"

She shook her head. "I'm sorry. I wasn't listening . . ."

Alfie soberly took Kristin by the hand. "I know you're not in any mood for horsing around. Let's you and I go nice and quiet to Haworth Olde Hall and those other two can follow."

For her part, Alexa was happy to be with the tall, handsome, if much too silent, Matthew. As they started down the steep hill, Alexa's heel caught and she stumbled. Matthew quickly put a supporting arm around her, and they continued that way down the hill to the old hotel.

When they got there, the restaurant and bar were empty. "See? Like I told you, this old place most certainly is not one of Haworth's nightspots. Not that there's any worth telling about." Alfie guffawed, then caught himself. "Follow me," he said in a hushed voice.

Now he led the way along a small brick path to the side of the building, where a large porch with French doors and curtained windows jutted out into the darkness.

"You just show me where Peter Flange told you the opening was." Alfie kept his hearty voice down. "Think you can locate it?"

Kristin surveyed the old house as best she could in the semidark. She tried to remember. She knew the metal grille was on this side of the building; she knew it was under one of the windows. But which one?

"I think it was one of those three windows," she told Alfie. As she pointed to them, two people came out on the porch and stood looking out through the curtains.

The four young people ducked for cover in the bushes. They could not see whether they had been spotted or not. They could only crouch there among the leaves and spiny branches of the thick greenery, holding their breaths, not daring to speak, praying they had not been seen. They waited for what seemed a very long time; then they heard a window close as a man's voice said, "Might as well turn in. Be sure to fasten that window, Alice. We're in for some more rain."

There was the sound of locks snapping shut and then footsteps treading the porch floor and disappearing.

After another long interval, Alfie said, "We can chance it now. Just hang in here while I have a look over yonder."

They waited anxiously as Alfie reconnoitered their surroundings. They heard a slight rustle of leaves, then silence, and then there came a soft, low whistle.

"That's Alfie," Matthew said.

They made their way over to a huge bramble bush. Behind it, Alfie stood, holding a pair of pruning shears with one hand, pushing the heavy bush back with the other, to reveal an opening in the side of the house about two feet from the ground.

"This is it. The entrance to the tunnel. I jimmied that metal slab down." He said directly to Kristin, "It's a filthy mess in there. Are you sure you want to come along with us?"

Kristin seized his arm and said violently, "We do! You can't keep us out!"

"Sssh! Keep it down, Kristin," Alexa said. There was a note of hysteria in Kristin's voice that frightened her. "Of course we're going with them."

"Well, all right," Kristin said, mollified.

One by one, with Alfie leading the way and Matthew bringing up the rear, they climbed into the dark hole. Inside, Alfie snapped on a flashlight to light their way.

"Are you going to leave that trapdoor open?" Matthew said.

"Aye, that we are. Say we get trapped inside, we can always make our way back here and beat it," Alfie said confidently.

"I hope you've got your head screwed on straight," Matthew said. "Lord only knows what we're getting into."

"Drop it," Alfie commanded him. To the others he added, "Now stay close together. I don't know when and where we'll be able to stand up, but it's crawling on our hands and knees until we find the spot." He reached out and took Kristin's hand, and said, "Stay in touch with my foot, there's a good girl. And you two follow suit, hands to feet, so we don't get separated."

They took off along a jagged, rock-hard crawlway no more than three feet by three feet. The earth smelled moldy, a smell of dead things, and yet not like any odor they had ever known. Not a living thing was in there — not a twig, not a plant, not an insect, not a rodent, not a snake. Nothing. They were four people making their way along a strange, black tunnel that seemingly led nowhere.

Their knees and hands were soon feeling the pain of pressing on the rough, unrelenting earth, despite the gloves on their hands, despite the slacks or jeans that covered their legs.

Kristin wondered at Alfie's assurance as he

made his way through the black into the unknown. But she stopped wondering when he suddenly spoke up.

"Now don't get discouraged. Do you hear? We should be getting to a stand-up space any minute." Then he added, "At least I think that's what'll happen. I've no way of knowing for sure."

Kristin thought, *I don't think he's telling the truth. Something's wrong.*

It was at that moment that they saw Alfie play the flashlight upward, and there was a much larger space in front of them.

"I say, Alfie," Matthew said as he and the others got to their feet, "you're a genius, d'you know that?"

"Shut up, you idiot," Alfie growled. "We don't know where we are, do we? We could be right under the Flanges' bedroom, you silly fool." His eyes gleamed dangerously in the dim reflection from the flashlight. He seemed transformed from the happy-go-lucky, perpetually joking Alfie they knew. Alexa flashed a look at Kristin and Kristin read it right, *I'm scared*, and flashed back, *So am I*. In the cold, dark deadness of the strange century-and-a-half-old abandoned tunnel, there was now an air of fear.

"Onward and upward," Alfie said blithely, as if aware of their feelings. "I don't know what's up there any more than you do."

Again Kristin wondered, *Is he telling the truth?* But then she thought of why they were there, of her hope that somehow, somewhere in this strange unearthly place, they would find some answer to the Brontë mystery that her mother had hinted at, that her mother was following when she disappeared.

There was nothing to do but warily follow behind Alfie, her hands clinging to the back of his jacket, Alexa's hand clinging to the back of her cape, and Matthew bringing up the rear.

What they would find ahead, God only knew.

How long they traveled in that hesitant way they did not know; Kristin could not see her watch in the dark, Alexa had left hers behind at the hotel; all they could do was follow Alfie.

After what seemed an eternity, he stopped.

"Now look at this," he said, flashing his light on a heavy wooden partition that blocked the passage. "I'm going to have a go at this. I want you all to stand back."

Matthew and Alexa retreated, but Kristin stood by Alfie. "No," she said. "I can't let you take this chance alone."

"Do you want to go back?" Alfie said. "It's either pry this thing open and see what lies beyond, or go back. There's no two ways."

"Isn't there any other way into these underground tunnels?" Kristin asked.

Alfie said slightingly, "Until you told me what Peter Flange said, I didn't even know this one existed. And I've lived right here in town my whole life."

"But Alfie," Matthew protested, "you're taking a chance of having the whole place cave in on us."

"Not the whole place," Alfie said, pointing to

the wood-beamed ceiling above where Matthew and Alexa stood. "There's a good support up there. If anything is going to give, it'll be in this section right here. I'd say the limestone down here kept everything in pretty normal condition. What's beyond that partition — that's what we don't know."

Kristin considered a moment, then came to a decision. "I want you to go back, Alexa. You too, Matthew. If Alfie is good enough to want to go on with me, it will be just the two of us. Why risk anyone else, if something does go wrong?"

"Now, Kristin —" Alexa began. But Kristin was adamant.

"No, Alexa. No! Now you two start back, and we'll wait until you're safely away before Alfie breaks down the partition."

She turned to Alfie. "You're sure you want to go on with me, Alfie? We don't know a thing about what's up ahead of us."

Alfie put up a hand. "Now don't you start that, Kristin. Of course I'm going on with you. Couldn't stop me if you tried." He turned to the others. "Get cracking, you folks. Mind you keep the entrance to the tunnel open back there, in case we have to give it up after all."

Alexa kissed Kristin tearfully. "Good luck, Kris. We'll wait just so long, and then we'll come after you. You can rely on that!"

With that, the two were gone. After a delay of three or four minutes, Alfie said to Kristin, "Step back!"

As she retreated a few paces, he rammed the

partition full force with his shoulder. Once, twice, three times. It did not budge.

"Let me help," Kristin said.

Before he could protest, she joined him in his next assault on the slab blocking their path, and it gave way!

"Nice work," Alfie said. "I needed that extra leverage."

Kristin was peering into the gloom ahead. Another quite different odor was coming at them in waves. Unlike the rarefied dead smell of the forward part of the tunnel, this scent told of living things. As Alfie flashed his light around him, they saw dark, ugly things scuttling away, squealing, clicking.

"Sure you want to keep on?" Alfie had a little self-assured smile on his face. "Could get a bit nasty, you know."

"Of course I want to go on," Kristin said. She gritted her teeth, and although the possibilities that lay ahead were terrifying, she vowed, *Nothing's going to stop me.*

Alfie shrugged and motioned her to follow as he led the way along the filthy tunnel with its overpowering scent. As she moved close behind him, Kristin felt fear and revulsion as she had never known before. Every now and then her flashlight caught in its beam a scampering, skinny black rat. Huge, dark brown water beetles and slugs scrawled their way along the walls; criss-crossed spiderwebs broke in their path, clinging to face and hair and hands, with no way of ridding oneself of them completely. Yet some kind of maniacal one-mindedness pushed Kristin onward, so that the dank, terrible journey seemed like a dream through which she was passing. At any other time Kristin — anyone — would have fled back to civilization, but this was now and if only this awful trip opened up some unknown path to her mother, wherever she might be, it would be worth everything. There was no turning back.

So busy was Kristin following Alfie, keeping her beam on the damp, rotting earth, that she was shocked to see he had come to a sudden stop. She raised her flashlight and a wave of terror rocked her as she saw his face. He was holding a thick, heavy, wooden club high above his head, and it was aimed at her.

"What are you doing?" she whispered.

The club in his hand moved closer as his eyes glittered with an expression Kristin could not fathom. "You'll see in a moment. I hate to have to tell you this, but I think it's all over —"

He never got to finish the sentence, for in that moment there was a low rumble, and dirt — a landslide — came pouring down on them.

The last thing Kristin saw was Alfie's astonished look as the dirt cascaded down in a curtain between them.

It was pitch-black. Kristin, her legs threatening to give way beneath her, reached down to see if she could find the flashlight she had dropped. She passed her palms along the dirt floor and ignored the squeaking of what seemed to be an army of rats as they frantically dashed for shelter away from the cascaded earth that had put a wall between Kristin and Alfie. Petrified of Alfie's violence, she nevertheless tried to make contact with him. Was he lying under the landslide? Maybe she could help him. She screamed, "Alfie! Alfie!" over and over, but there was no answer. She could not turn back, there was only one way for her to go — straight ahead along the hideous, rat-infested tunnel. It might lead anywhere, it might collapse at any other point; but she had no choice. She started to make her way along the ground when suddenly her foot kicked something. Her flashlight! She bent and picked it up and flicked the switch. It worked! Gratefully, she hurried along the tunnel, grateful that the light frightened the rats out of her path.

Now the exhaustion was coming upon her again. How long she traveled in that long, dark, rotting tunnel, she did not know. It was when she finally thought she had to quit that she saw a pale glimmer of light perhaps ten feet ahead. She stopped, turned off her flashlight, and let herself be led by the dim glow in front of her. She tiptoed stealthily toward it, stopped, listened, heard nothing. She ventured ahead once more. This time there was the tread of footsteps behind her. Before she could spin about to see what it was, there was a *whush* of something above her head. Before she could utter a sound, something cracked down on her head and she dropped soundlessly to the ground in a senseless heap.

CHAPTER 15

It was very cold. And the light was dim. She stirred on the hard floor and was shocked to discover that she was bound hand and foot.

More of the nightmare. *It can't be.* But it was. Her hands were tied together at the wrists behind her back, and the rope led down to her feet, which were tied at the ankles. There was a piece of cloth tied over her mouth, but she turned her head to her shoulder several times and easily displaced the cloth. She could breathe freely, but her heart pounded so thunderously in her ears that she heard nothing else.

Where am I?

She could have called out, but instinct told her not to. She looked around and saw that she was in a small stone-walled room with one tiny opening, like an airspace in a dungeon, through which daylight was coming.

How did I get here?

Then she remembered. Her race down the tunnel, struggling up the hill to Top Withens, standing in the doorway and then, nothing.

Who did this to me?

And more important, the next question in her mind — *Why?*

A shadow fell across the wall and she looked up to see a face that was familiar. It was the blonde woman who had danced at the party in the Pink Heather! The same girl Richard had chased after outside the Chinese restaurant in Chester!

What is she doing here? What does she want from me?

"Here, let me help you." The blonde girl was bending over her, patting her cheek comfortingly. "Who did this? How terrible! I'll have you free in a minute."

Kristin whispered, "Thank you," as the blonde loosened her bonds. She rubbed her hands together to get the circulation back, then stood up painfully as thousands of needles in her legs prickled her blood along its accustomed paths.

"I'm Pamela Ruthven." The blonde thrust her hand out. "I'm an ornithologist. Birds, you know." She hesitated. "I'm the fiancée of a young man whom you know. Richard Fayne . . . ?"

"I — I don't know him very well," Kristin said, cautious, her heart lurching. *Is it true?* she wondered. It would explain so much.

But the blonde was indicating a butterfly net she had dropped on the floor. "It's not cricket to entrap a bird, but sometimes I have to. To get data I need." She smiled charmingly. "Who are you? How did you come here?"

Kristin looked into the girl's dark brown, shining eyes and saw a strangeness there. *I've got to watch my step. What can I tell her? I'm not going to tell her the truth.*

Then it came to her — what it would be safe to say.

"My name is Alexa Bower. Don't expect me to tell you how I got here." She shook her head sadly. "Someone knocked me down. I don't know who." She shrugged and looked at the coiled rope. "I thought maybe you could tell me something."

The blonde girl said, "No, I know nothing about it, Alexa." She cleared her throat. "You're American, I see. May I ask what you are doing up here in Yorkshire?"

The lie came easily this time. "I'm an archaeology student. A freshman at Columbia University — in New York City. You've heard of it?" Pamela nodded and Kristin went on, "I was wandering the moors, looking for some relics — stones, pottery, anything the Romans might have left behind —"

"You were looking in the dark?" Pamela said suspiciously.

"I lost track of the time," Kristin said. "Then when I found myself near this building, I thought I'd go in and rest a bit before I started back to town." *Will she believe this?* She forced a laugh and said, "You're a scholar, I can see that. Didn't you ever get carried away with your work?"

Pamela Ruthven smiled. "I certainly have. As a matter of fact, Alexa, I come from a family of very talented women."

Kristin said tentatively, "It must be something in the Yorkshire air. I mean — those other talented women, the Brontës. Fantastic, weren't they?"

A cloud passed over Pamela's face. "They're not the only ones. There were others, you know."

Kristin, certain now that they were on dangerous territory, said, "Well, I'll let you be the expert on them, Pamela — and on the birds, of course." She smiled ingratiatingly. "I'll try to be the expert in archaeology."

Pamela's face was smooth again. She said, "You must be hungry. I have some food in my knapsack. It's not very special — some bread and cheese. If you'll wait here, I'll go and get it." She paused. "You'll wait right here?" Kristin nodded. "Good. I'll only be a few minutes." And she was gone.

Kristin's brain raced. *She's very strange. I don't know what she's up to. When I said, "Brontë" she went berserk for a minute. She knows something about my mother. I know it. I know it!*

She saw a second doorway in the room. Into her mind flashed, *Act. Focus. Dare to do!* It was taking a big risk, but this was no time to be careful. She ran across the doorsill, swinging her flashlight to see where it led.

She got reckless as she moved along now, hurrying so that Pamela would not find her searching this way. Her foot missed the floor and struck a stone step. She reached for the stone wall but could find nothing to grasp. She slid down several steps and landed on a stone-cold floor, hurting. But she got up, painfully, in the dank blackness and flashed her light again, stumbling from one dungeonlike room to another. Rats, gray ones, fled before the flashlight's beam. She pushed on and on.

And then she saw it. A patch of black in the corner. Straw spread around it. A bundle of rags? It was hard to identify. There was a white blur — a face?

She whispered softly, "Mother?"

She started ahead, when a hand rudely grasped her shoulder and yanked her across the floor.

It was Pamela Ruthven, enraged, her features twisted into devastating hatred. Kristin recoiled from that horrifying spectacle — a madwoman with bloodshot eyes, fingers clutching her in a paralyzing grip that hurt so badly she cried out in pain.

"You *liar*! You *cheat*! Like *she* is! You're her daughter! Well, I've got you both now." She laughed evilly. "Only she's dead. And soon you will be!"

In a moment, they were locked in mortal combat. Kristin fought with every ounce of strength at her command. Desperation, the need to survive, surged through her body and lent her force beyond force. But it was not enough for the wild ferocity of her attacker. Try as she would, Kristin could not shake the demented creature off. They wrestled their way along a wall. Kristin lost her footing and, falling, dragged Pamela down with her. As they landed on the floor, Kristin was appalled to see Pamela's hair brush against the candle's flame. In an instant, her blonde hair was on fire.

"I'll help you!" Kristin yelled, tearing her cape off and running toward Pamela. But the madwoman, her face distorted, a hideous mask of hate and agony intermingled, raised her two hands, her two bare hands, and tore at the flaming hair — and it came off!

Pamela hurled the bright blonde wig to the ground and stood there, laughing and screaming at once, shaking a full head of raven-black tresses down to her shoulders.

There a stranger stood — black-haired, wild-eyed — beating her hands together — a creature from a fantasy world, a world of terror. Kristin saw again the dancing figure on the moors and knew the two were one and the same.

"See, see me now? See Fiona Brown, daughter of the Brown dynasty! The cream of Yorkshire! See my beautiful black hair? Like my ancestor, Eunice Brown! My whole family robbed of fame and fortune by the filthy Brontës! By the Brontës, who stole our work and said it was theirs."

She let out a shriek and leaped at Kristin. Kristin grabbed the madwoman's arm as it came around her throat from behind. That arm was steel, throttling her.

"You're my enemy, like your mother!" A burst of maniacal laughter.

Kristin could not breathe in that viselike grip. She tore at Pamela's arm but could not dislodge it.

"Too late! You've come too late, you poor fool! There she lies in the corner . . ." She turned Kristin toward the darkest corner of the room where Kristin had first seen what looked like a heap of rags.

"Too late!" In her exultation, Pamela loosened her grip a little, unintentionally. Kristin, sucking in an enormous gust of air, gained momentary strength.

"She wouldn't do what I wanted," Pamela said. "So now she's dead." Her voice became a high childish treble. "I took good care of her, I did! But she dragged it out too long. Not my fault!"

Kristin, shocked to her marrow, looked at that still face in the corner — she could see it more clearly now — and saw to her horror that it was indeed her mother.

Frantic, she tried to break away, to go to her, but it was hopeless. Pamela, her dark hair falling over Kristin's face, obscuring her vision, drew her iron arm tighter and tighter about Kristin's throat.

I've got to do something. I can't die like this. Not here, not now. My mother — She felt a blackness descending over her. Her vision blurred and she could have dropped, but she would not let go. She had to do something.

With a monumental surge, she lifted a foot and kicked behind her with all her might at Pamela's shinbone.

Pamela shrieked with pain and let go. Taking in deep lungfuls of air, Kristin sidestepped the madwoman and sought an opening. Sought and found it. As Pamela bent to clutch her injured leg and rub away the pain, Kristin raised both hands above her head and brought them down violently on the back of Pamela's neck. To her astonishment, Pamela dropped and lay prone on the cold stone floor, unconscious.

She ran across to where her mother lay. By the now very dim glow of the candle, she saw the beloved face. Her mother, but not the face she knew. It was cold, white, and not a muscle moved, not a stirring of life of any kind.

She reached over and touched her mother's hand. It was ice-cold, clammy.

She could keep silent no more. The word was wrenched from her innermost depths.

"Mother!"

Not a sound, not a flicker of an eyelid from the black-clad figure on the floor.

She fell on her knees, kissed her mother's cold cheek again and again, and cried, "Mother! It's me, Kristin!"

She raised her mother's hand and it fell lifeless to the floor.

CHAPTER 16

Kristin was crying hysterically now. She seized her mother in her arms and held her tight. *I've got to get her out of here.* Crazy thoughts spun through her mind. *I won't let them take you away from me. I won't. We're in this to the end, Mother. Mother, I love you. Don't go away now.*

I've got to get you out of here.

Even as she thought this, she heard it. A sound. A sound that came closer and closer as she waited there in the dark, holding her mother's limp form. Closer, closer . . .

Voices.

A man's voice, as footsteps rang swiftly on the stone floor outside and in the next moment, figures bursting into the room.

Flashlights lighting the darkness — and Kristin saw them. Alfie! Matthew! Alexa! Maurice Whalley and his wife, Peggy. And behind them a tall imposing figure — a familiar figure even in the dark. Richard!

Two of them swiftly unrolled a stretcher. Before anyone could speak, there came from Pamela a low moan, the sound of an animal in pain. Quickly Richard, seeing her injured on the floor, was beside her.

He looked at Kristin, who nodded. "She tried to kill me, Richard. I had to fight back. My mother . . ." She bowed her head to the body in her arms.

In an instant, Alexa was by her side. "You found her! Kristin, you found her!"

Then, anxiously, Alexa peered at the still form. "Oh no. Oh, no! Don't tell me . . . your mother . . . is . . . is —"

Richard ran to Kristin's side and raised her mother's eyelids. He put his head to her chest, then put his finger in the small hollow of her throat.

"I'm afraid she's gone," he said.

Kristin screamed, "No! NO!"

She pushed the others aside and yelled, "Alexa! Help me! C.P.R.!"

Alexa dropped beside her as Kristin bent down, parted her mother's lips, and began mouth-to-mouth cardiac pulmonary resuscitation. While Kristin breathed regularly in and out, in and out, Alexa pressed Margaret Clark's ribcage and then released it with a spring, pressed and released, again and again in a regular rhythm.

"*Do it!*" Kristin said urgently, between breaths. "*Do it*, Alexa! We won't let her slip away. Not now!"

Fiercely the two girls worked in the dark, as the others stood by, watching. Watching and waiting. Without hope.

Then, as the minutes rolled by, as perspiration poured from their faces, their bodies, the dim candle beside Margaret Clark flickered out.

As it did, Margaret's chest heaved by itself, and she took in a deep breath. She was alive.

"You got there just in time," the surgeon was saying. "You saved her life. We can save the leg, I'm ninety percent certain we can."

Kristin and Alexa were in the corridor outside of Professor Clark's room. It was a small but excellent hospital with a highly talented staff.

From where they stood, Kristin could look in on her mother, who was sleeping in an immaculate white hospital bed with a clear-view plastic oxygen tent over the upper half. "To ease the strain there's been on her heart," the doctor had assured Kristin. "She'll be good as new with the proper care. And we'll see that she gets it here."

Even so, Kristin could hardly stand to let her mother out of her sight. She'd had a brief visit to the bedside, where she'd kissed her mother and seen her radiant smile, then left.

"She needs rest," the doctor was saying now. "Let her sleep. Come by and see her as often as you want, but only for a few minutes. Rest, sleep, and good food will make her well."

As Kristin and Alexa left the hospital, Richard Fayne was waiting outside.

"Good morning," he said. "How is the patient doing?"

"According to the doctor, great," Alexa said.

"But he won't let anyone spend any time with her."

"In that case," Richard said, "I'd like to take you two for a bit of elevenses at a tearoom down the street. Do I hear 'aye'?"

"Aye, aye," Alexa said.

"And you, Madame?" he asked Kristin.

"Fine with me," she said. She felt uncomfortable with him and was glad Alexa was there.

Inside the tearoom, Richard ordered scones and jam and hot tea ("It's raining out there, for a change," he said), and then he leaned back in his chair and was silent.

"What I can't understand," Kristin said, "is where you came into it." She looked directly at Richard. "You knew Pamela Ruthven?"

"It's not her name." Richard took a scone and spread it with jam. "She's Fiona Brown. A very sick woman. She has spent a good part of her life in a mental institution. Matter of fact, she just got out of one six weeks ago. That's why I went after her. When I learned that she was probably the one who took off with your mother, I dropped everything and went looking for her."

"She said you were her — you were engaged to her," Kristin said.

Richard said, "Fiona and I are related, Kristin. Legally, not by blood ties. She's my second cousin once removed. My grandaunt — by marriage — had Fiona late in life, after my granduncle died. My father always felt a responsibility toward her. Some members of her family believed they were cheated by the Brontës. They said the Browns wrote the Brontë books. Actually, there was a Eunice Brown who worked as a housekeeper for the Brontës. But these Browns have no connection to her."

"My mother went off with her," Kristin said. "Pamela must have given her a very convincing story."

"Oh, they're brilliant, those Browns. But completely unstable. Fiona was beyond that — totally aberrated about the Browns and the Brontës." Richard looked at Kristin. "She *escaped* from the mental hospital, Kristin. That's why I couldn't let you in on Fiona's real identity. She'd have killed you without a second thought if she knew who you were. I had to keep you apart as I tracked her down."

"You did a good job of it," Kristin said. "I thought you were a pretty suspicious character yourself. I didn't know what you were up to — I just felt you weren't leveling with me."

"I wasn't," Richard said. "Actually, I didn't know who you were till we met in Edinburgh. I had gone down to London, thought I'd do the museum and see some plays and look in on your mother at Daley's. They told me she was expected there. But then I got a call from the university in Edinburgh and had to rush up there on school matters for the coming term. An emergency."

"But Chester? What happened there?" Kristin asked.

Richard smiled. "By that time I was on your mother's trail and trying to look after you at the same time, to see you didn't get into trouble." He said ruefully, "I didn't do a very good job of it, I'm afraid."

"And the time you left me at the Chinese restaurant?"

"By then, of course, I knew that it was Fiona your mother had left the school with, although I tried to keep the information from you. For your own sake." His eyes twinkled warmly at her. "Did you out of a meal, didn't I?" Then he sobered and said, "When I saw Fiona passing by, I thought I had her at last. But she got away."

"What was she doing in Chester?" Alexa asked.

"She'd learned from your mother that possibly there was information in Chester that she could use to back up her claim, so she left Haworth and came down by herself. When she saw I'd spotted her, she left town immediately."

"I still don't understand everything. I really don't. What about the Whalleys?" Kristin asked curiously.

"Haworth people look after their own," Richard said. "It's like Oriental people do. The Chinese always say, when one of their own has done wrong, 'No need to call police. Chinese people are police for Chinese people.' Same thing with us Haworthians."

"I thought you came from Scotland?" Alexa said.

"I was born and raised in Haworth, Alexa. Spent my upper school years in Scotland." He grinned. "Nosy little twosome, aren't you?"

Kristin said, "Well, there's still a lot more I

need to know." She stood up. "I want to go up to our room and get some things for my mother. She hasn't a decent thing left. I want to bring her perfume and a couple of personal items, and a present I brought from home . . ."

"Then we'll walk you back to the good old Hillside Hotel," Richard said. "We'll wait for you."

"You bet," Alexa said.

Ten minutes later, they were at the front stoop of the dilapidated hotel.

"No need for either of you to come up," Kristin said. "It's a gorgeous day. I'll only be a minute."

"Are you sure. . . ?" Alexa said.

"Sure, I'm sure. I'm A-okay. So's my mother. So's everything. What could possibly go wrong now?"

She walked through the tired little room that was the TV lounge to the rear. As she started down the long narrow corridor that led to her room, she saw a shadow. She continued on, hesitating. Who was it? Another guest? The maid? A stranger?

She stopped. Her heart pounded as the shadow moved out of a niche and resolved itself into a solid mass — a man.

Farouk Kalemi!

Before Kristin could say a word, he seized her and put his hand over her mouth. Then he dragged her several yards to the utilities closet out of which he had stepped.

"Be quiet, Kristin, if you want to go on living." He kept his hand over her mouth, but she could breathe. The air in the little closet was stifling.

So that's it, she thought. *He's the one. The one who's been following me, wrecking my room, breaking into Alexa's place at the Quadro, ripping into my suitcase.* A terrible sadness overcame her. *He's the one, and I never suspected it.*

She stood there, desolate, thinking, *It can't be.* After all they'd been through — this terrible, terrible time that she and her mother would never forget, they were safe. It was all safe again — safe and more wonderful than ever before. And there was Richard . . . No, there was nothing. Not now.

Farouk loosened his left hand, still covering Kristin's mouth with his right. He shifted her to his right side and reached for something in his pocket. Kristin knew before she saw it what it was — a revolver.

From outside, there was the sound of a creaking door opening. Farouk threw the closet door wide and flung Kristin toward the rear of the closet, Kristin heard Farouk say, "Get your hands up! You're covered! If you make one move, you're a dead man!"

Kristin, clinging to the side wall of the closet, made her way to the door.

What she saw there surpassed belief. A thin, frightened, blue-eyed, blond rat of a man.

Harold, the English steward from the airplane.

CHAPTER 17

Farouk Kalemi snapped a pair of handcuffs on the angrily cursing English steward as Kristin watched in disbelief.

Farouk Kalemi took an ID card out of an inner jacket pocket and flashed it before the steward's anguished eyes.

"Chief Inspector Kalemi of the Egyptian international secret police," he identified himself to his captive. "It is my duty to warn you, Harold Evans, that anything you say may be held in evidence against you."

At the police station, Kristin, Alexa, and Richard stood by as the steward was charged in an indictment.

"Don't worry," he snarled at Farouk Kalemi, "you haven't got anything on me!" He was between two guards, who tried to restrain him.

"Oh, but we have," Inspector Kalemi said. "Your confederate at Kennedy airport in New York has implicated you as his European pickup man."

"The filthy swine! He messed it up! He gave

the wrong signals!" Hands handcuffed behind him, he twisted toward Kristin, in a fury. "They said it was in your bag! What you've cost me and the others can't be counted!" His voice rose to a shriek. "Where-did-you-put-that-picture-frame! Where? *Where?*"

"Picture frame?" Kristin said. "Oh, you mean this one?" She reached into her purse and pulled out the double oval that held the two pictures of her mother and herself. "This?"

Farouk Kalemi held out his hand and Kristin handed him the encrusted silver frame. Kalemi took a small pocket knife out, and after studying the frame and the pictures, began to pry gently away at the back. The pictures came loose from the frame, and many small packets dropped into his palm.

"We'll just open these little bags inside and identify the contents. I'm quite sure," he said to the police captain, "that there's enough pure, uncut drugs in these packets to make them worth several hundred thousand on the continent."

The steward, howling with rage, was led away.

Outside the police station, Farouk Kalemi took Kristin's hand as Richard and Alexa watched.

"You're quite wonderful," he told her earnestly. "I hated leaving London so abruptly without word for you, Kristin, but that steward is part of a very active, very dangerous drug smuggling crew. It wasn't easy trailing Evans and his friends without letting you in on what was up. If they had any idea that you knew their game, your life wouldn't have been worth sixpence."

Kristin shook her head. "They were the ones breaking into my room at the Daley, Alexa's room at the Quadro, slitting my bag at the inn at Chester?"

Farouk said, "None other. Evans was told the stuff was dropped into the back of a picture frame in your bag at Kennedy. He couldn't find the picture —"

"It was a present for my mother, Farouk. When I got to London and the trouble about her not arriving began"— she swallowed, remembering — "I put it in my purse and carried it with me all the time." She stopped. "Of course! That's why he was trying to get my tote bag away from me on the plane — to check that out first!"

"Right. If it was in the tote, he'd have removed it neatly, taken the contraband out, sealed up the back, and you'd never have been the wiser. When it wasn't in the bag, they went after your room at Daley's. The rest you know."

He consulted his watch. "I'm on the run now." His huge dark eyes surveyed her. "It's been a joy to know you, Kristin."

Impetuously, she reached over and kissed him on the lips and held him. As she did, she saw Richard striding off quickly, followed by Alexa.

"You should have seen the look on your face," Alfie said to Kristin. "You thought I was about to do you in. Confess now, didn't you?"

They were all seated in the Red Lion Inn — Richard, Kristin, Alfie, Matthew, Alexa, with the Whalleys laying out a splendid luncheon spread "on the house, you know," and tying up all the ends.

Kristin said, in reply to Alfie, "I'm sorry. But there you stood, with that club raised up above your head and looking at me in that funny way —"

"It's my face," Alfie said. "I can't always get it to look the way I'm thinking. I was only trying to tell you that I'd heard a rumble and felt a sprinkle of dirt, and I tried to raise the club to hold off whatever was about to come down on you."

Kristin reached over and grabbed his hand. "You're the best, Alfie. A prince. And don't knock your face — it's wonderful." Which caused Alfie to blush joyfully.

"Then I owe you an apology, Kristin girl," Maurice Whalley said. "I didn't want you hearing too much, nor Peggy making a big fuss about the tunnels. I'd made up my mind to go down and have a look and see if there was a sign of any human life down there." He stood tall. "If your mother came to grief in Haworth, it was for us to right it, you see."

Richard and Kristin exchanged glances. *I told you*, his eyes said. *I know*, hers responded.

"And now it's my turn," Peggy Whalley said. "I didn't give you enough credit, Kristin. I thought, why bother the girl's head, she's worried enough, I'll take her mind off it —" She broke off and looked faintly ashamed. "As if anything could! We've no children, which is why I treated you like a child, instead of a woman."

"Please," Kristin said. "Everyone has been

absolutely wonderful. You're the best people I've ever met. I can never thank all of you enough." She radiated happiness. "And it's all turned out so well. My mother's going to be able to leave the hospital in another week, and everything's back to normal."

"Well, mark my words, Kristin," Maurice Whalley said somewhat heavily. "You've shown us all what a woman, a very *young* woman, can do. With no ifs, ands, or buts, you got an idea in your head, you followed it through past any place where anyone else would have given up, and you alone made it work." He gulped and looked surprised. "Why, you're the equal of any man I've ever known!"

"Hear, hear," said Richard. "Coming from you, Maurice, it's like being knighted. In Kristin's case, being made a Dame of the British Empire."

He looked at her warmly. *In a friendly way,* Kristin told herself. *He's a friend, that's all.* It made her sad.

On the way back to the Hillside Hotel, Richard managed to take Alexa by the hand and urge her ahead of the others, which left Kristin behind with Alfie on one side and Matthew on the other.

Well, it figures, Kristin thought. In the end, Alexa had that old-fashioned, feminine something that men wanted. Maybe they felt safer with that kind of woman. The kind she was not. *After all that's happened, it's Alexa he wants.*

"I say, Kristin," Alfie said, as they stopped in

front of the little Hillside Hotel, "we've got to say our good-byes."

She pulled herself back to the present. "Alfie, Matthew." Before she realized what she was doing, Kristin reached up and kissed Alfie solidly. She released him and reached for Matthew and did the same.

"There," she said, her eyes shining. "I couldn't help myself. I like you both so much."

"Now be sure you keep in touch," Alfie said huskily. "We'll want to hear from you, Kristin."

"We do," Matthew, the silent, spoke up. "Once you're back home, we'll be waiting to hear from you."

They said good-bye to Alexa and Richard and left. Kristin, seeing Richard and Alexa resume their private conversation, started up the stone stoop.

"I've got some packing to do," she said, not looking at either of them.

"Kristin, wait up," Alexa said. "There's something you have to settle for Richard and me."

"Yes?" Kristin said tonelessly.

"You tell her," Richard said to Alexa.

Here it comes, Kristin thought. *Big news from the happy couple.*

"Richard wants to make plans for Christmas," Alexa said happily. "He's got a vacation coming and he wants to come to the States."

"That sounds okay," Kristin said. "What's the problem? You've got plenty of room at your house, Alexa."

"It's not my house he wants to visit," Alexa said.

"Thanks, Alexa, I guess I'll have to do this myself." Richard cleared his throat. "What I'd like to do, Kristin, is come to America on holiday. I would like to get to know your mother." His brown eyes locked into hers. "It would mean a lot to me."

Kristin looked from Richard to Alexa. Alexa nodded her head, her eyes shining with mischief.

"It seems only fair," Alexa said, "You visit Richard's country, now he visits yours."

"Alexa," Richard said softly, "would you mind if Kristin and I left you for a little while?"

"Not at all." Alexa looked up at the sky, a magic blue-black dome pinpointed with silver stars strewn around a deep orange harvest moon. "It's a lovely night for a walk on the moors." She waved her hand gaily and disappeared into the hotel.

Richard said, "How do you feel? Think you'd like a little stroll on the moors?"

Still unbelieving, Kristin said, "I would, Richard."

He took her arm and they strolled slowly back up the hill, past the Red Lion Inn, and up the narrow country road that led to the moors. How different it was from that day she had come up here alone, penniless, and hungry, that dark day only two weeks before. Now the moor was an all-embracing haven, offering not danger, but peace and warmth.

They walked all the way in silence, savoring the heather-scented air, the beauty of the night.

Following some unbidden impulse, Richard led the way and stopped beside the waterfall outside the very cave where Kristin had spent that awful night.

"Kristin, Kristin. If you knew how I've waited for this . . ." He drew her closer, and she raised her lips to his.

That kiss was everything she remembered. It promised love and tenderness and commitment. She did not tell him how long she had waited for — and never expected — this moment, too. There would be time, much time, to tell him everything.